A Grave

Blackmoore Sisters Cozy Mystery Series
Book 6

Leighann Dobbs

2

This is a work of fiction.

None of it is real. All names, places, and events are products of the author's imagination. Any resemblance to real names, places, or events are purely coincidental, and should not be construed as being real.

A Grave Mistake
Copyright © 2015
Leighann Dobbs
http://www.leighanndobbs.com
All Rights Reserved.

No part of this work may be used or reproduced in any manner, except as allowable under "fair use," without the express written permission of the author.

Cover art by: http://www.coverkicks.com

Chapter One

This wasn't the first dead body Morgan Blackmoore had seen, nor was it the most gruesome, but for some reason *this* body struck ice-cold fear into her heart like none of the others.

It wasn't the look of terror frozen on the guy's face, or the giant burn mark on his chest indicating he was probably a victim of some kind of paranormal assassin that had her so frightened.

It was the map clutched in his fisted hand … a map that looked eerily similar to one Morgan and her sisters had received in a mysterious letter from their Aunt Eliza.

Morgan bent at the waist, her sleek, long black hair dangling in front of her as she strained to get a closer look.

Was it the same map?

It looked like it, but she didn't have the photographic memory her sister Jolene did, so she did the next best thing. She slipped the cell phone out of her pocket and snapped a picture.

As she leaned in, something gooey squished under her boot. Picking her foot up, she recognized it as one of the cone-shaped, black licorice candies they sold in the corner store—a Black Crow.

"Hey, Morgan. Do you mind?" Brody Hunter pulled her attention from the smooshed candy and she straightened to see him standing behind her in his Noquitt police uniform, holding up a section of yellow crime scene tape so that it was high enough for someone to duck underneath. He jerked his head toward the area outside the tape, indicating for her to leave. She took one more quick photo, then slipped under the tape.

"Thanks." She tweaked his cheek and smiled as he blushed. She'd known Brody most of her life. They'd both grown up in Noquitt and, since he was the younger brother of Morgan's high school boyfriend, she thought of him like family.

Her smile faded as she walked away, glancing down at the photo of the map on her phone. She snugged her black pea coat around her middle to ward off the cool November air but it did little to stop the chill that crept from her spine and encircled her heart.

She glanced back one more time, wondering who, exactly, the body was. She knew that the possession of the map indicated they must have come to her seaside town of Noquitt, Maine, for a specific reason. A specific reason that had gotten them killed.

What she didn't know was if the dead person was friend or foe ... or if the killer was still hanging around town.

Morgan picked up the pace, her breath coming out in small puffs of condensation, her boots making tracks in the light dusting of snow on the ground, as she hurried to her truck.

She wasn't sure exactly what was going on, but if her theory about the map was correct, things in her little town were about to heat up dramatically despite the late fall New England weather.

She hopped in the truck, turned the engine over and put the truck in gear. She didn't let it warm up—she needed to get back home with her discovery and warn her sisters.

On the way out of town, the reflection of flashing blue and red lights in her mirror caught her eye. Glancing behind her, she saw them load the body into an ambulance. Her stomach clenched. She had a feeling that might not be the last death this town would see before the year was out.

***

Celeste Blackmoore brushed a light dusting of snow off the bench at the edge of the cove. Shoving red leather gloves into her pocket, she sat down and pulled the lobster grilled cheese from its bag, watching a wisp of steam rise in the air.

Settling back on the bench, she closed her eyes and bit into the warm sandwich. It was a favorite of hers and one that she'd only been able to find at *Foot Bridge Lobster*, a small lobster shack situated in Perkins Cove, which was a short walk from her home.

The sandwich had the perfect combination of taste and texture. Grilled bread gave it a buttery crunch, the cheese added creamy tang and the large lobster claw situated in the middle supplied the perfect amount of sweetness.

Celeste sighed as she settled back on the bench to savor the sandwich. Although it was less than forty degrees out, she didn't mind. Celeste found the cooler weather invigorating and she loved her seaside town even more in the off-season, when it wasn't crowded with tourists.

She chewed happily, looking out over the quaint fishermen's cove. The light dusting of snow would be gone by noon, but right now, it gave the place a holiday feel, amplifying the charm of the old lobster boats moored in the cove.

But not all the boats had charm. Especially not the big, black ship moored in the middle that stuck out like a sore thumb. Celeste stared at the ship, the sandwich paused halfway to her mouth.

When did that get here?

A feeling of uneasiness bloomed in her chest. Noquitt was a popular tourist destination in summer and sometimes people rented mooring space to stay in the cove on their boats, but no one ever did that in winter.

Yet, here was this big, black boat and obviously someone was staying on it. She watched as a figure appeared on the deck. It was two people, actually, one dressed in a Nordic parka and pushing a tiny, white-haired woman bundled in a light-blue blanket in a wheelchair.

Celeste watched as the woman turned her face toward the sun. She looked frail, sickly. The woman reminded Celeste of her mother, who had been held captive by a maniac for the past seven years and drained of almost all her health. Thankfully, her mother was recovering, but Celeste couldn't help but wonder about the woman she was looking at now. Had she suffered a similar fate?

Finishing the rest of her sandwich, Celeste watched as the woman was wheeled back inside and the door to the cabin shut, blocking any view she might have had of what was going on inside. Maybe the woman was just here convalescing and recovering?

Celeste brushed the crumbs from her hand, chastising herself for being so suspicious. She never used to be that way, but the past two years had been crazy for her and her sisters, who'd discovered they'd had special paranormal gifts and then come under attack because of them. She'd learned to pay attention to anything out of the ordinary.

She stood, and with a glance backward at the boat, started for the large house she and her sisters shared with their mother at the mouth of the entrance to the cove. There was no reason to be suspicious of a new boat in the cove, but she'd keep it in the back of her mind. As Celeste had so recently found, it was better to be safe than sorry.

Chapter Two

The Blackmoore house had been in Morgan's family for centuries. Built three hundred years earlier by Morgan's ancestor Isaiah Blackmoore, it sat on a piece of land with the Atlantic Ocean on one side and the channel to Perkins Cove on the other. The house, now more of a mansion, had started off as a small home and been added to and modernized with each passing generation.

Morgan pulled to a stop in the driveway and followed the smell of eggs and bacon into the spacious kitchen, her jaw dropping when she saw a tall, dark and handsome guy at the stove cooking the breakfast.

"Mateo! What are you doing here?" Morgan's eyes drifted from Mateo's velvety brown ones to her mother, Johanna's, amber ones.

Johanna shrugged. "He came to visit."

"Bet you didn't know I could cook," Mateo said, turning his broad shoulders back to the stove. Morgan *hadn't* known that cooking was one of his talents and her lips curled as she wondered how her youngest sister, Jolene, would react when she found out who was preparing breakfast.

Mateo had been somewhat of a mystery man, appearing out of nowhere on several occasions to rescue the sisters during the past year. Unbeknownst to them, he had actually been working for a secret agency and was tasked to watch over them. Morgan didn't think he minded that task, especially when it included her sister, Jolene. She'd seen the way the two of them looked at each other and, even if neither of them wanted to admit it, there were sparks there.

Recently, they'd discovered Mateo had been on an assignment inside the underground laboratory of Dr. Mortimer Bly, a rogue paranormal who had held her mother prisoner for seven years trying to drain her powers. Johanna and Mateo had developed a strong friendship and he'd been instrumental in rescuing her.

That probably explained why he'd just popped in unannounced to cook breakfast ... or maybe he wanted an excuse to see Jolene.

"Is something wrong?" Johanna asked.

Morgan had been so surprised to see Mateo, she'd almost forgotten about the body with the map. Almost.

She held up the phone. "I think the relic we've been searching for might be a little closer to home than we originally thought."

Mateo spun around. "Really?"

Morgan nodded and showed them the picture.

"That looks like the map Eliza sent." Johanna's lips pursed into a thin line and Morgan worried that her mother wasn't strong enough yet to deal with something like this.

When the sisters had received the mysterious letter in the mail, they'd tried to keep the map from their mother. But Johanna had been adamant about being included in the task of searching for the ancient relics that Dr. Bly was trying to uncover for his own evil purposes.

According to what they'd been told, these relics had been infused with paranormal powers by energy masters centuries earlier and anyone who possessed them would be able to use the power for their own gain. Morgan's aunt Eliza had sent them a map which they'd assumed was a clue to one of the relics. Too bad she hadn't indicated where, exactly, the map pointed to. Morgan and her sisters had assumed it was someplace ancient … like Egypt or near the Mayan ruins. But now that someone had shown up in town with the map, that seemed to indicate they were looking for the relic here in Noquitt.

Morgan studied her mother, who sat in her wheelchair, head bent studying the map. For seven years, she'd thought her mother was dead. They'd been led to believe Johanna had jumped into the sea from the cliffs behind their home. It was a miracle to have her here now. And she was getting stronger every day.

When they'd first rescued her, she'd been unable to walk, her skin had been as wrinkled and brittle as someone almost three times her

15

mother's age. Her long hair had been a dank gray —almost devoid of color.

Now, Johanna's hair showed streaks of its normal jet black, her skin was smooth and she could manage to get out of the wheelchair and into a chair and bed on her own.

Johanna's mind was as sharp as ever and in the few short months she'd been back, it had become obvious to Morgan that her mother was the leader of the group. She could handle this.

"Yes, I thought so, too," Morgan said.

"Where did you get this?" Mateo held the greasy spatula up as he leaned over the phone.

"I was at the Village Food Market downtown picking up a few things when I noticed flashing blue lights on Beach Street. Normally, I don't pay attention to police business, but my gut instincts told me to investigate." Over the past year, Morgan had learned that her gut instincts were a special gift and she always paid attention to them.

"Someone was killed and they had the map?" Johanna asked.

Morgan nodded. "It looked like they were burned. Probably with paranormal energy, but I'm sure the police will explain it as something else."

"Too bad you didn't snag the map," Mateo said.

"Brody kicked me out. I was hoping the picture was enough."

"We should print it out and compare it to the one from Eliza. Email it to me." Morgan did as instructed while Johanna wheeled her chair around and headed for the sitting room next to the kitchen where they kept a printer and laptop.

"What's burning?" Jolene appeared in the doorway, her brown hair tussled like she'd gotten out of bed without bothering to straighten it. Which she probably had. Her light blue eyes grew wide as she noticed Mateo who had turned his attention back to the stove in order to rescue the bacon from being burnt to a crisp. "Uh-oh, this can't be good." Her brows crept up as she glanced at Morgan for confirmation.

"Well, I don't know if Mateo cooking breakfast is good or not, but I did make a discovery downtown that isn't so good."

"Oh?"

"She found a map," Mateo said, his back still turned.

"And you think it has something to do with Eliza's map?"

"It looks pretty similar."

"Let's see." Jolene held out her hand and Morgan handed the phone over.

Jolene squinted, then used her finger and thumb to enlarge the picture.

"It is the same, but it looks like there's an additional part to this one," she said with certainty. Morgan believed that certainty. Jolene had a photographic memory and if she said it was the same as the other map, you could take that to the bank. "Let me go get the one Eliza sent us."

"So what does this all mean?" Johanna wheeled over with the printout of the map and put it on the shiny, granite surface of the kitchen island.

Morgan looked down, tilting her head sideways to see it from a different angle. It wasn't the full map—part of it was inside the dead guy's curled fingers. "I'm not sure, but if someone was here with the map then that seems to indicate they were looking for something right here in Noquitt."

Jolene returned with the other map, laying it on the island next to the printout. "So, the relic Eliza was trying to lead us to could have been here under our noses the whole time?"

"Maybe."

Morgan looked at the two maps. They *were* almost the same. But she didn't recognize it as anyplace in Noquitt. She was studying it so intently that she didn't hear someone enter the kitchen.

"Hey, who cooked breakfast—"

18

Celeste stood in the doorway, staring from the platters of food Mateo was placing on the kitchen island to Mateo, then to Jolene.

Her eyes slid back to Mateo. "Hi. I didn't know you were here."

"I just dropped in to see how Johanna was doing."

"Uh-huh." Celeste took a piece of bacon off the pile and nibbled on the end. "Did someone say something was right under our noses?"

"Yes, I found—" Morgan started, then stopped. They were missing one sister and she didn't want to have to tell the story all over again when Fiona showed up. "Where's Fiona?"

"Outside, practicing her shotgun rocks." Johanna jerked her head toward the big kitchen window and Morgan looked out to see her sister standing just outside, her right hand clenched in front of her in a tight fist. Fiona's back was to them. A lavender, knit scarf warmed her neck and kept her red hair tucked into the back of her tan, shearling jacket. Beyond her, the Atlantic Ocean sparkled in the morning sunlight.

Two years ago, the sisters had been attacked by paranormal bad guys who had been after a treasure Isaiah Blackmoore had hidden in caves beneath the house. That's how they'd discovered they'd actually had paranormal abilities themselves. Since then, there had been more attacks and the sisters had decided to hone their skills so they could be more effective in defending themselves.

Fiona had a way with crystals and Morgan knew Fiona hoped to develop a skill where she could transfer energy to the small stones and then throw them as weapons, causing them to scatter like shotgun shells which would pepper the enemy senseless.

Morgan held her breath as she watched Fiona raise her fist. Then she flung her hand out, her breath visible in the cold air as her fingers flew open and the stones clattered harmlessly to the ground.

"Looks like she still needs some practice," Celeste said.

Jolene tapped on the window to catch her sister's attention and motioned her in.

Fiona came in through the kitchen door, stomping her feet and blowing into her ungloved fists.

"What's up?" Her eyes slid to the island. "Oh, great. Breakfast's ready."

"Yeah, that and Morgan came across a dead body this morning," Jolene said as she loaded scrambled eggs, bacon and toast onto a plate.

Fiona's left brow inched up. "Another one?"

Morgan rolled her eyes. The sisters had found more than one body in the past couple of years

20

and it was starting to be a family joke. Except usually, they were the ones getting blamed for the death.

"Yeah, at least we aren't suspects this time." Morgan slid the printout of the photo she'd taken across the island toward her. "He had this in his hand."

Fiona tilted her head to look at it as she shrugged out of her coat. "Is it the same as Eliza's?"

"It looks like it." Jolene set the picture next to the map they'd gotten in the mail as they all filled their plates and sat around the island.

"See, this part matches, but this part looks like a continuation," Jolene said around a mouthful of egg.

"What's that?" Celeste pointed to a rectangular object on the corner. "It looks like a gravestone."

"I think it is." Jolene slathered butter on a piece of toast and held it out to Celeste, who shook her head.

"You're not eating, dear?" Johanna's eyes clouded with worry. "Are you sick?"

Celeste laughed and pointed to the take-out bag she'd tossed in the trash. "No, I ate already. My favorite—lobster grilled cheese.

Morgan screwed up her face. "For breakfast?"

"Sure. It has all the things you are eating." Celeste pointed to the various plates on the island.

"Protein, dairy and bread. I got it at the Foot Bridge. That's when I saw the boat."

"Boat?" Johanna, Morgan and Fiona all asked at once.

"Yeah. A big, black boat was moored in the cove. Odd for this time of year."

"I'll say," Morgan said.

"I don't think that's a coincidence," Johanna added. "Maybe our dead guy came from there."

Celeste pursed her lips. "I don't think so. There was an old woman in a wheelchair. At least I *think* she was old." Celeste couldn't help but glance at Johanna.

"Or she could have been a victim of Bly, just like Johanna," Mateo said. "Do you think Bly might be here?"

Morgan reached for a piece of bacon. "Hard telling, but someone paranormal is. The dead guy was killed with hot energy."

"We should check that boat out," Jolene said. "But first, we gotta figure out what this map means."

"*Meow.*"

Their cat, Belladonna, glared at them reproachfully from the doorway as if she was wondering how they *dared* eat breakfast without her.

Belladonna sauntered over to the trash barrel, stood on her hind legs and sniffed. Then she stretched to reach her head far enough in so that she could peek inside the bag. After a few seconds, she pulled her head out and slitted her sky-blue eyes at Celeste, clearly annoyed with her for not saving even a morsel of lobster. She then gave the final insult by trotting over to Mateo and sitting adoringly at his feet.

Mateo broke off a tiny piece of bacon and held it out for the sleek, white cat, who sniffed it thoroughly before gently taking it with her teeth.

"I don't think she should be eating bacon." Jolene frowned at Mateo.

"She likes it." Mateo shrugged, then cleared some of their empty plates from the island, putting them in the sink so they could study the maps side by side.

"If this is Noquitt, I don't recognize it," Fiona said.

"*Mew.*" Belladonna clawed at Mateo's pant leg and he tossed her another tiny piece of bacon.

Jolene turned both maps to face her. "It looks like this is the ocean." She pointed to the right side.

Celeste stood and leaned over the island to see what Jolene was pointing at. "Then you must be holding it upside down, because if it's Noquitt, the ocean would be on the east side."

"*Merow!*"

"Shush, Belladonna." Morgan waved at the persistent cat to shoo her out of the room, but the cat stayed, stretching her neck out as if she was trying to see to the top of the island where the plate of bacon was.

"I don't know," Jolene said. "I think the orientation is right. Maybe this isn't Noquitt."

"*Meowww!*" Belladonna jumped up on to the island. Sliding across the length, she grabbed a piece of bacon in her mouth on the way by. Her claws caught on the photo of the map and sent it fluttering off the side as she leaped off the end of the island. She landed almost silently on the floor and then darted out of the room.

"Hey, you!" Fiona yelled after the cat amidst laughter from Mateo, Celeste and Jolene.

Morgan bent down to pick up the printout of the picture she'd taken earlier that morning. The printout had twisted around and lay upside down on the floor. As Morgan reached for the paper, Johanna's hand shot out and stayed her arm.

"Wait a minute. I think I know where this is."

Chapter Three

"I don't know why we can't just go out to the Finch farm and look around. No one's lived there for years, since Thaddeus Finch went into the nursing home," Jolene complained from the backseat of the gray TrailBlazer the girls had recently purchased.

Fiona half-turned from her position in the passenger seat so she could see Jolene. "That would be trespassing. Mom was right. We need to ask old Mr. Finch's permission first."

"You're just crabby because Mateo left." Morgan glanced at Jolene in the rear-view mirror to see her sister's reaction to the good-natured teasing.

Jolene snorted. "Where did he run off to, anyway? And what brought him here?"

"Who knows?" Celeste shrugged. "He's mysterious. But I have to say I don't think his appearance and a dead body showing up on the same day are coincidence."

"Yeah, but if so, why did he *leave*?" Jolene asked.

"Good question," Morgan replied as she pulled into the *Fiddlers Rest Nursing Home*.

"I hope Mom is right about the map being the old Finch farm, or this is going to be a huge waste of time. I hear Mr. Finch doesn't even make sense most of the time." Jolene held the glass door to the lobby open and motioned for her sisters to precede her. "He might not even know we are here, never mind be aware enough to give us permission to look around his farm."

"Can I help you?" a nurse asked from behind the round desk, just inside the carpeted lobby.

"We'd like to visit Thaddeus Finch," Morgan said.

The nurse's brows rose. "Looks like it's Mr. Finch's lucky day. He doesn't usually get so many visitors."

"So many?" Jolene asked.

"Yes, his nephews were here earlier."

"Maybe we should come back, then?" Fiona looked at her sisters questioningly.

"Oh, they're gone now. I'm sure Mr. Finch would love to see you. He's in room three-ten." The aid leaned around the desk and gestured to a hall on the left. "Just take the elevator over there and follow the signs."

Thaddeus Finch's room was bigger than Morgan had expected. It was about fifteen by twenty, painted in a nice gray blue with a hospital bed in the middle, a wooden bureau on one wall, a big television and a large window overlooking the woods in the back of the facility.

Finch sat in a recliner in the corner. He was a small man, with a mop of bushy, gray hair. A hand-crocheted afghan in shades of orange and green spread across his lap gave Morgan the impression that Thaddeus was cared for by at least one person. Maybe his nephews.

Fiona tapped on his door, pulling his attention from the television. His gray eyes lit up when he saw the four girls hovering in the doorway.

"Finally you're here to give me my bath." Finch started taking off his shirt, much to Morgan's dismay.

"No. No." She waved her hands. "We're not here to give you a bath."

"No?" Finch's face collapsed in a disappointed frown. His eyes flitted from one girl to the next, then settled on Celeste. "Are you sure? I always was a sucker for blondes."

Celeste ran her hands nervously through her short-cropped, blonde hair. "We're sure."

Finch settled back in his chair. "Why *are* you here, then?"

"Now, Mr. Finch, are you being naughty again?" A young woman with strawberry blonde hair pulled back in a severe pony-tail appeared at the door that led to the room's private bath.

"What?" Thaddeus squinted at her. "Potty? No, I don't have to go potty."

The girl shot an apologetic look at Morgan and her sisters, then held her hand out. "I'm Wendy, Mr. Finch's personal health aide."

They introduced themselves and then Wendy said, "Don't mind me. I'll just straighten up over here." She turned and headed toward the bedside table, her thick, waist-length hair swishing and flying as if it had a mind of its own.

"Well, hello there!" Thaddeus said brightly as if he'd just noticed Morgan and her sisters. "What can I do for you lovely girls?"

"We have a favor to ask. About your farm," Morgan said.

Finch smiled. "My farm. Yes. I love that place. Been in the family for generations, you know. Of course, lots of Noquitt homes have." He stopped, then frowned at them again. "Who did you say you were?"

"We're the Blackmoore girls," Morgan said. "Morgan, Fiona, Jolene and Celeste."

"Oh, yeah. I'd recognize you anywhere. I knew your grandma and you girls have the same eyes," Finch said, referring to the sky-blue eyes, a Blackmoore trait the four girls were lucky enough to have inherited. Finch's eyes clouded and he looked out the window, then back at the girls. "Are you here to give me a bath?"

"No," Morgan said. "We'd like permission to look around your farm."

"Oh, well I haven't checked for eggs yet."

"Excuse me?"

"The hen-house. I haven't been out there yet. But if you girls want to look around go ahead."

"Well, that's okay. We were actually interested to see if there was a family graveyard."

"Oh, yeah." Finch rolled his eyes. "Scary thing to have in your back yard when you're a kid growing up on a farm. Don't make a grave mistake, my great-granddaddy used to say. He's buried there, you know."

"Oh, that's nice." Jolene jerked her head toward the door in a signal to her sisters that it was time to go.

"Yep. My grandpa is in there, too, and my daddy. 'Course I had to get special permission to bury them there." Finch's face turned sad. "I wonder if I will be buried with them. Probably not. No one left to get special permission."

"What about your nephews?" Morgan asked.

Finch looked at her, confusion spreading across her face. "Nephews? I don't have any nephews."

Chapter Four

"I know he *said* he didn't have any nephews, but he's loony tunes. He probably doesn't remember." Jolene's eyes were on her cell phone, her thumbs flying over the letters on the popup keyboard as they picked their way through the overgrown area surrounding the Finch farmhouse. "We can't just assume his earlier visitors were Bly's men. I mean, he thought we were there to give him a bath, so I don't think he's really in touch with reality."

"True. I guess we need to check that out," Celeste said. "Who are you texting?"

"Jake. I want to tell him to check out that boat you saw in the cove," Jolene said, referring to Jake Cooper, ex-Noquitt cop and Jolene's private investigator boss as well as Fiona's boyfriend.

"Good idea." Fiona's ears had perked up at the sound of Jake's name.

"Which way do we go?" Celeste turned in a slow circle, taking in the large area. The farmhouse with its peeling paint and hanging shutters was dirty from years of neglect. What had once been a front lawn was a mass of tall grass, turned brown for the winter. To the right was a field ringed by a fence dotted with broken boards. Next to it, a barn had fallen down decades ago and lay in a mass of boards and shingles. Beyond that

31

sat another pile of debris, a few pieces of charred wood sticking out from the edges.

"If Finch does have nephews, it looks like they don't take very good care of the place," Morgan observed.

"I guess Finch didn't, either. How long has he been in the nursing home?" Celeste asked.

"I'm not sure, but you know how old people get. They stop taking care of things. This place looks like it's been going to ruin for thirty years." Jolene held up her cell phone that showed an old picture of the farm from better days. "But it's a prime piece of land. Twenty acres edged by the ocean to the east and the woods to the north."

Fiona frowned. "If he had nephews, wouldn't they be keeping it up? It was in his family all these years, it doesn't make sense it would just be going to ruin."

"Lots of young people can't be bothered with keeping a farm running. They probably plan to get rid of it, but can't sell until Thaddeus dies."

"Speaking of dying," Morgan said. "Let's find this graveyard."

They started off toward the back of the farmhouse. The noon sun had warmed the day to the mid-forties, and Celeste took off her gloves and shoved them in her pocket as she walked.

Beside her, Morgan slowed her pace, her eyes narrowing as she scanned the horizon. Celeste could see her homing in on a spot and the three sisters waited until Morgan pointed to a hill that backed up to a wooded area. "That seems like a likely place."

They started toward it at a faster pace now, the shapes of gravestones becoming more visible as they approached.

The old graveyard sat in a rectangular area built up on the top of the hill. It had a great view of the ocean, which Celeste thought was ironic seeing none of its inhabitants would be able to enjoy it.

The family plot was large. Ringed by a black iron fence set in a footing of concrete, the area had been built up higher than ground level and the girls ascended three moss covered concrete steps to get inside.

"Now what?" Jolene asked.

Morgan shrugged. "I guess we look for a clue."

The graveyard turned out to be bigger than it appeared at first. A lot of Finches had been buried there and it was as overgrown as the rest of the farm, which only added to its creepiness. A gigantic, thick old oak tree sat almost dead center, its bare branches spread out several feet in all directions, and Celeste imagined the dark canopy it would create in summer when it was full of leaves. Some of the older slate stones had cracked in half, their tops laying on the ground or leaning up against the remaining part of the stone.

The girls' pace slowed as they inspected the stones. Morgan took the lead and when she slowed and put her hand out, the rest of them stopped.

"What is it?" Celeste's neck tingled with awareness. Did Morgan sense someone watching them?

"I thought I saw someone." Morgan nodded toward the woods.

Celeste squinted in that direction, but all she saw was tree trunks. "I don't see anyone."

"Maybe it's his nephews," Jolene added.

Morgan shrugged and turned away from the wooded area. "I'm probably just jittery. Let's keep moving, but stay alert. We don't want to get surprised in an attack."

Celeste turned her attention toward the graves, scanning for anything that might be a clue. The stones themselves were mostly older. She guessed the ones in the back dated to the 1700s when family plots were more common. Two stones near the front were newer and she assumed those belonged to Finch's father and grandfather.

The older stones were the most interesting. Some were plain, slate slabs, rounded at the top and chiseled with images of angels, weeping willows and doves. A few of them in white limestone had images in high relief. Celeste paused to run her fingertips over the gritty surface of an angel's wings on one of the stones.

"So, what exactly are we looking for?" Celeste asked as she studied the stone.

"Good question." Jolene looked around. "Got any vibes, Morgan?"

But Morgan was busy staring at something behind them.

"Huh?" Morgan spun around to face them.

"Jeez, you're making me nervous." Fiona bent down and scooped up a handful of stones, closing her fist around them for a second then opening it up a little and peeking inside. Celeste could see disappointment on her face, but Fiona closed her fist and kept the stones inside.

"Do you have any sixth sense about where to look so we can narrow down our search?" Jolene asked.

"I don't. I guess we should spread out and see if there is a clue on any of the graves."

"What about the mausoleum?" Fiona angled her head toward a cement doorway that was lower than the main graveyard and set into a mound of earth on the East side. It was small and not terribly ornate. The giant, iron hinges that held the doors shut, and the fact that it was inside the earth, made entering it a less than appealing prospect.

Morgan shook her head. "I don't think the clue is in there. Besides, it's clearly locked ... and it looks creepy inside."

"Yeah, let's stick to looking around out here first, then maybe we can look in there." Jolene glanced over at the structure. "That lock looks easy enough to pick."

"It would help if we knew what kind of clue we were looking for," Fiona said as the girls started to spread out amongst the graves.

"No kidding."

Celeste immersed herself in looking at the graves, searching for anything that stuck out. What would the clue be? One of the images engraved into the headstone? Some wording in one of the epitaphs? She tuned everything else out while she searched, moving deeper into the cemetery.

In the back of the cemetery, Celeste could see a couple of chest tombs, their rounded tops making them look like concrete coffins sitting above ground. The stones back here were more ornately carved, as were the tombs.

A wispy mass swirling from behind one of the stones caught her eye and she sucked in a breath. She recognized the swirling shape ... it was a ghost.

"'Bout time you got here," the ghost said.

She shouldn't have been surprised to find a ghost in a graveyard and it didn't startle her as much as it might have. Celeste was getting used to seeing ghosts—she'd been seeing them for a while now. Talking to the dead was her special gift.

"You knew I was coming?" she asked the wispy swirl that was now solidifying into the shape of a man.

"Of course. I been here a long time with Henry and Red." The ghost nodded toward one of the ornate chest tombs. This one had a flat top and Celeste noticed two other ghosts sitting around it as if it was a table. They held something in their hands. Cards!

Her brows mashed together as she squinted at them. "Are they playing poker?"

"Yep. We got our regular poker game going so I don't have much time, but you girls better take good care of that special item ... I tried to keep it safe when I was alive."

"Oh, right. And just what is this special item?"

The ghost looked at her slyly out of the corner of his eye. "Oh, come on. I know you girls know about it. Otherwise, why would you be looking?"

"We need to keep the relic away from the bad guys."

"Yes, of course. That's no secret. You'll know it when you see it and know what to do with it."

"Yes, but what, *exactly,* is it?"

"Why, it was one of my prized possessions. You do know who I am, don't you?"

Celeste shook her head.

"Well, I might have been a bit before your time. I'm Ezra Finch. One of the very first pharmacists here in the state of Maine." The ghost puffed up in a swell of pride. "People came from all over the country to get my medicines." He leaned in close to Celeste and winked. "Some say they were magical."

"Magical?" Celeste's brows shot up.

Ezra laughed. "Sure. You know what I mean?"

"Sort of," Celeste said. "So, where can we find this relic?"

Ezra's thin, ghostly lips pressed together. "Well, I can't say where it is now. I don't leave the graveyard here, and I know there's been some changes since my time. But be that as it may, I provided a clue before I left this world."

"Okay." Celeste was starting to feel impatient with the ghost's vague talk and wondered if senility ran in the family. "What's the clue?"

"Why, it's in the center," Ezra pointed toward the middle of the graveyard. "The most important part of the graveyard, of course."

Celeste glanced in that direction. All she saw was rows of gravestones. "Could you be more specific?"

"Specific? You want me to spell it out?" Ezra glanced at his wrist. "I'd love to but I don't have time. I gotta get to the poker game. The boys are waiting, though I do wish we had a fourth. Anyway, you girls should be smart enough to figure it out, and if you can't, then maybe you aren't the ones it should be entrusted to."

And with that, he turned and walked off toward the now-empty chest tomb poker table, his ghost fading with each passing step. When he was almost invisible, he turned back and said, "Oh, I almost forgot. Don't make a grave mistake."

Celeste could hear the echo of his laughter as he slowly faded into thin air.

"What is it?" Jolene asked. The others respected Celeste's unusual gift of talking to ghosts and had learned that when it looked like she was talking to no one, it usually meant she was talking to the departed. They'd learned to be quiet and let her do her thing.

"I'm not sure. I might have just talked to a senile ghost, but he seemed like he knew we were looking for a relic and he pointed me this way." Celeste pointed her finger in the direction Ezra had indicated.

Jolene and Celeste started in that direction with Morgan and Fiona following. The center of the graveyard was easy to find. It had stones back to back in a square with a large black obelisk in the middle, about fifteen feet from the trunk of the big, old oak.

"What are we supposed to be looking for?" Fiona asked.

"That's the problem. My ghost friend was very vague." Celeste bent down to inspect one of the gravestones. "Maybe it's one of these epitaphs."

"They are fascinating," Jolene said from behind one of the old stones. "Like this one. *We must all die, there is no doubt. Your glass is running, mine is out.*"

"How about this one," Fiona chimed in. "*Thou lovely child in parents hope, in early years cut down. Companion now of the ghastly group, that lie beneath the ground.*"

Morgan made a face. "Those are depressing. I don't see a clue in either of them. Do you guys?"

They shook their heads, then Morgan added, "Did your ghost give you anything more specific? I mean, we could be looking at these graves all day and not find a thing."

Celeste shrugged. "He just said it was the most important part of the graveyard and not to make a grave mistake."

"Don't make a grave mistake?" Jolene repeated. "Thaddeus said that, too. He said his great-grandfather used to say it."

"That's who my ghost was, I think." Celeste looked down at gravestone of Ezra Finch. He would have been just old enough to be Thaddeus' great-grandfather."

The others came to stand beside her. "Looks like he's got a snappy saying on his, too," Fiona said. *"When two become one, the healing's begun. In my favorite place under the sun."* She moved closer to the stone, squinting at the bottom. "This line is harder to read ... *Look to the west, I can finally rest*."

"That makes sense he would talk about healing," Celeste said. "He was quite proud he was one of the early Maine pharmacists and said people came from all over for his medicines, as they had powerful healing properties."

"Like Morgan," Fiona pointed out.

"Yeah. Maybe he had paranormal powers, too," Morgan said.

"That would explain why he had the relic, but I don't see how this gravestone could give us a clue," Fiona replied.

"Wait a minute," Jolene said. "I don't think it does. You said he said it was in the center, right?"

Celeste nodded.

"And then he said *don't make a grave mistake*, right?"

"Yeees." Celeste drew out the word.

"Well, don't you guys see?" Jolene flapped her arms. "It's not on the graves. It's on this obelisk which is probably in the exact center. Looking at the graves is a *mistake*."

Celeste felt a spark of hope. "Yes! That makes perfect sense."

The obelisk was one foot wide and four feet tall. It was made of smooth, black marble. The three sides were flat, like a long, thin triangle. It was topped with a round ball.

Too bad Celeste didn't see any clue on it.

The four girls circled the object a couple of times.

"Okay, I don't see any clue," Fiona said finally.

"Well, it's not going to be obvious." Jolene's voice rose in exasperation. "If it was too obvious, it would be too easy for anyone to find the relic. We have to use our brains."

Jolene bent down to brush dirt away from the bottom of the obelisk and Fiona rolled her eyes.

"It's always something cryptic," Fiona muttered as she bent closer to the sides of the obelisk, which were polished smooth on the edges but had a rougher pattern engraved down the middle. The pattern reminded Celeste of a Celtic knot, but not exactly. As she stared at it, she realized it looked familiar.

"Hey, I think I've seen this pattern before." She ran her hand along the pattern, feeling the bumps of the carving with her fingertips.

42

Fiona came around to stand beside her. "Hey, you're right. I think this same pattern is on the Oblate Museum building. Don't you think, Morgan?"

But Morgan wasn't paying attention. She stood in a rigid line looking toward the woods across the field, like a springer spaniel sighting a bird.

Celeste looked over in time to see the sun glint off a glass surface. Someone was watching them with binoculars.

"Stop right there!" Jolene barked as the four sisters took off running in the direction of the intruder.

***

But the intruder didn't stop. Which pretty much ruled out Thaddeus' nephews. Surely, they wouldn't be running away from intruders on their own land?

Morgan ran as fast as she could. Beside her, she could see Fiona trying to keep up, her fist clutched around the pebbles. Up ahead, the figure weaved its way west—toward the road. He had a good head start and he was fast.

Morgan willed her legs to go faster as she tried to gain on the person. It was a man, she thought, but she couldn't get a good look while concentrating on running and trying not to whack into any of the trees. He looked to be average height, and was wearing a thick, hooded sweatshirt so she couldn't see his hair. It would be all but impossible to recognize him later.

The man was getting close to the edge of the woods and Morgan figured he probably had a car parked on the road. They'd need to catch up pretty quick if they wanted to stop him. "He's getting away!"

"There's no way we can catch him before he gets to the road," Celeste huffed between breaths.

"Maybe I can slow him down," Fiona yelled.

Out of the corner of her eye, Morgan watched Fiona pull her arm back then fling it forward, releasing the stones she'd been holding. Morgan held her breath as the stones bounced ineffectively off the trees. No magic there. Fiona's face crumbled in disappointment and Morgan's heart pinched for her.

Jolene took a cue from Fiona and thrust out her palms. A stream of purple energy shot out, but too many trees were in the way. The energy hit a pine tree, splitting in in half. The two halves fell away from each other and landed with a thud. Morgan jumped over one of the halves and continued forward.

A few seconds later, the girls burst out onto the road just in time to hear a car squealing around the corner. They'd lost him.

"Damn it!" Jolene stood in the road, staring in the direction of the car.

Celeste bent over at the waist to catch her breath and puffed, "Who was that?"

Jolene turned back to face her sisters. "Someone following us."

"Or watching us," Fiona said.

"Well, I know one thing," Jolene added. "Whoever it was wasn't a paranormal."

"How do you know that?" Fiona gasped as she held onto her right side.

"Because if they were, they would have just used their paranormal powers to fight us or escape instead of running."

Celeste straightened. "Maybe they weren't supposed to capture, just observe us."

"You mean let us do the detecting work and then swoop in at the end and take the relic?" Jolene nodded. "That sounds like something Bly would have his men do."

"That's for sure." Morgan blew out a breath and kicked at a stone on the ground. Looking down, she noticed something that sent a jolt of recognition to her brain. She bent closer and nudged at the object with her toe. Her heart froze as she watched it roll off the pavement into the sand on the side of the road—it was a Black Crow licorice, just like the one she'd seen next to the dead body.

Chapter Five

Jolene wrapped her fingers around the mug of steaming hot chocolate and leaned toward her sister Morgan, who sat opposite her in the oversized chair in the East sitting room of their home.

"So, you think whoever was watching us was the same person that killed the guy with the map?" she asked Morgan.

Morgan nodded. "They're definitely linked, somehow. I can feel it. And how many people eat those licorices, anyway? It's too much of a coincidence."

Jolene glanced out the large bay window, with its panoramic view of the Atlantic Ocean below the cliff only a couple of hundred feet from the home. It made sense, except for one thing—the guy they had seen hadn't used any paranormal powers. But maybe he wasn't trying to capture them or hurt them—just because he didn't use the powers didn't mean he didn't have them.

One thing was for sure. Whoever killed the guy with the map was after the relic. And now, it looked like he was after them, too.

But who was the killer? One of Bly's men? A rogue paranormal? Or someone else altogether? All they had to go on was a piece of candy and a dead body.

"Is there any word on who the dead guy was?" Jolene settled back on the couch and looked up at Luke Hunter, Morgan's boyfriend. "Maybe if we can figure out who he was, we can get a bead on who was following us."

"I'm one step ahead of you on that. I asked Brody and he said his name was Hale Swain."

Fiona tapped her fingernail on her pursed lips. "Hale Swain ... that name sounds kind of familiar."

"Are you thinking of Gunner Swain, the archeologist?" Celeste asked. "I've heard Cal mention him a few times."

"Maybe. Do you think they are related?" Fiona asked.

Celeste shrugged. "Who knows? But what's an archeologist got to do with any of this?"

"Good question. And Swain isn't exactly a unique name. It may not be related, but maybe we should check into this archeologist guy." Morgan turned to Luke. "Did Brody say if the police have any leads or any idea why this guy was in town?"

Luke shook his head. "Not really. They think he was killed with some kind of new-fangled taser in a bar fight."

Jolene snorted. "I guess they would. They don't know about paranormals."

Luke knew about them, though. He knew all about the Blackmoore sisters' abilities. In fact, that's why he'd come back to town in the first place, after spending two decades in military service. He hadn't known it at the time, but his new job with a secret government agency was designed to keep him close to the Blackmoore sisters. A happy side effect of that was that he'd reconnected with his former high school sweetheart, Morgan.

The girls had learned that keeping their 'gifts' a secret was wise, so they didn't tell many people about them. That included Luke's brother, Brody Hunter, who happened to be a member of the Noquitt police force. They figured what he didn't know couldn't hurt him.

Fiona leaned forward on the couch, her red curls sliding across her arm as she put her cup of tea down on the coffee table. "Do you think whoever was following us could have figured out the clue on the obelisk?"

Morgan shook her head. "I doubt it. They weren't in hearing range. All they would have known was that we were looking at the obelisk as well as the gravestones."

Celeste's brow creased. "What I don't understand is if he was following us, then how did he end up at the nursing home *before* us? And the aide implied there was more than one person."

"Maybe that really *was* his nephews at the nursing home." Jolene turned to look at her mother and she felt a flood of warmth. For years, she'd resigned herself to the fact that she'd never see her mother again and now here she was, sitting across from her looking happy and on the way to good health. "Do you know if Finch had any nephews?"

The room they were in had been her mother's favorite and they'd continued to use it even after they thought she was dead. But, for Jolene, using the room had been bittersweet. Her mother's touch was evident throughout the decor, from the soft blue and gray colors to the giant starfish and shells, to the chippy, white-painted furniture. On the one hand, the room had made her feel closer to her mother, but the constant reminder that Johanna was gone had always made her heart ache.

Seeing Johanna sitting in this very room with Belladonna curled up and purring in her lap was something Jolene never thought would happen, and the sight of it still made her heart sing.

Johanna shook her head, her long, silvery hair swinging like silk. "No, he was the last of the Finch family line."

"Speaking of the Finches, I talked to Ezra Finch—well, Ezra's ghost—and he seemed to know we were looking for a relic," Celeste said.

Johanna pressed her lips together. "Ezra ... he was before my time. Your grandma would remember, but I think he was famous for something."

Celeste nodded. "He said he was a pharmacist and his pills had almost magical healing powers. I think he might have been a paranormal."

"That makes sense. That's why he would have a relic." Luke twisted up the side of his mouth. "What exactly *is* the relic, anyway?"

Jolene sighed. "That's one of the problems. We have no idea."

"Gonna make it kind of hard to find, isn't it?"

"Yeah. We don't have too many leads except the obelisk in the graveyard."

"And you think that's a clue to the Oblate Museum because the pattern on the side matches?" Luke asked.

"Yep, I looked them both up on the internet," Jolene said, then in a lower voice, added. "Even though I didn't have to."

"But that doesn't make sense. The Oblate Museum has only been around for five years ... there's no way Ezra Finch could have put a relic there because he was already dead," Luke pointed out.

"The *museum* has only been open for five years, but the building has been there since the early 1800s. It was there when Ezra was around. Back then, it was a grange hall." Johanna petted

Belladonna's silky fur and the cat let out a little meow as if in agreement with what she'd just said.

"But if Ezra hid a relic in there ninety years ago, wouldn't someone have found it by now?" Morgan asked.

Jolene shrugged. "Maybe. But maybe he hid it really well. We don't have any other leads, so we have to follow this up."

"Well, then, I guess I know where we'll be going this afternoon," Morgan said.

"Yep, we'll be making a visit to the Oblate Museum."

Chapter Six

It was Jolene's turn to drive, so they all piled into the TrailBlazer and made their way to the Oblate Museum across town. Fiona sat in back, her stomach swooping as she noticed the blue flashing lights parked in front of the old building.

Celeste peered out the window as they pulled to a stop. "What's going on?"

"I don't know, but we better find out." Jolene jammed the car into park and they piled out, running up the steps and right into Brody Hunter.

"Whoa." Brody held his hands up in front of him, stopping them at the top of the steps. "Where are you guys going?"

Jolene craned her neck to see around him. "What's happening in the museum?"

Brody's eyes narrowed. "It was robbed."

The sisters exchanged a look. "Robbed? What did they take?"

Brody looked at them sideways. "Why do you ask?" He turned to Morgan. "And is it a coincidence I keep running into you at crime scenes?"

"Yes," Morgan said dryly, then added, "Is the museum terribly damaged? Can we go inside? I'd like to talk to the staff."

"If you weren't practically married to my brother, I'd be suspicious, but as it is, I'll let you go inside. The area is cleared and they want to open for business, anyway."

"Thanks." Morgan pinched his cheek and Fiona saw him turn pink before shaking his head and walking away.

"This can't be a coincidence," Jolene said as Morgan opened the glass doors for them to enter the foyer of the museum.

The large foyer had an oversized, oak desk at one end. Bernadette Mayhew stood in front of the desk in a light brown cardigan and pink and brown plaid skirt. The four foot tall senior citizen had to be ninety if she was a day, but she was feisty as all get out. Fiona didn't know who to feel more sorry for—Bernadette, or the thieves that might have tangled with her.

"What happened?" Celeste asked.

Bernadette pressed her lips together and said in a startlingly loud and clear voice, "Vandals, that's what happened. They broke right in at the noon lunch break and messed up the displays. Hooligans, that's what they are."

"In broad daylight? Was anyone hurt?" Fiona asked.

"No. We run on a skeleton staff in the off-season. I was the only one here today and I closed up for my noon break. Had to go pick up some new orthopedic shoes. When I came back, the door was open and it was a mess out back."

Bernadette waved her hand toward the back of the museum.

"Can we see?" Morgan ventured.

"Sure. I'll show you. Thankfully, they only messed with one display." Bernadette turned and started toward the back. She looked over her shoulder at the girls. "I must have scared them off when I came back."

"Did you see them?" Jolene asked.

"Not really. I think they ran out the back when I came in the front. I thought I heard the door back here bang shut."

The museum was just two rooms. The old grange hall had been divided into the front foyer, with a tall divider wall and openings on either side leading to the large back room which was sectioned off into the various museum displays. Along the back wall were bathrooms and a small kitchen, which looked to Fiona like it could be the original from the grange days.

The building still had the original, wide, pine-plank flooring that groaned as they walked, adding an eerie feeling to the quiet building. Bernadette stopped in front of a display with smashed glass and empty spaces where the stolen items must have been.

"Is this the only display that was messed with?" Morgan turned to look around the museum, the rest of which seemed to be in place.

Bernadette nodded her gray head vigorously. "Yes. They took old apothecary jars, and mortars and pestles. She leaned toward them and lowered her voice. "Probably for one of those mess labs."

"Mess lab?" Celeste asked.

"I think she means meth lab," Jolene said.

"Yeah, whatever ... you know how young kids are these days." Bernadette looked at Jolene and flushed. "Sorry, I didn't mean *you,* Jolene. Anyway, these items were priceless, from the early days of Maine. We had one of the very first pharmacists here—Ezra Finch. His family donated the things in this display."

Fiona looked at Bernadette. "Did you say Ezra Finch?"

Bernadette's face lit up at a chance to talk about Noquitt history. "Why, yes. He was an herbalist just like Morgan, and one of the first to produce medicine using chemicals. Of course, that was before they even had pharmacists, but that's what the discipline evolved to. Back then, pharmacists made their medicines in an apothecary and Ezra had one right on the Finch farm. It was the only one in Maine and people came from all over to get his medicine."

Fiona's brows knit together. "I didn't see an apothecary on the Finch farm."

"It burned down many years ago." Bernadette shook her head. "Anyway, I must have scared the vandals off before they could loot any of the other displays."

"Well, it's a good thing you weren't hurt," Morgan said.

"I admit, it was a bit disturbing, but it takes a lot more than some young yahoos to hurt an old bat like me." Bernadette cocked her ear toward the foyer. "I think I hear more visitors. I best go greet them and explain about the mess. You girls take as long as you want to look at the displays."

Fiona watched her bustle off, then turned back to look at the damaged display, her stomach sinking. "So, it looks like they got to the relic before us."

"I don't think so," Morgan said.

"What do you mean? This stuff was from Ezra Finch and something is missing. The relic is obviously one of the things they took."

"No. That doesn't make sense. Ezra hid the relic, so how could it be in the museum? He was already dead when they turned the grange hall into a museum."

"The relic was probably in the stuff his family donated," Celeste offered.

Morgan twisted her lips. "Maybe, but my gut tells me otherwise. Plus Ezra told Celeste he'd *hidden* it."

"Well, I know enough by now to trust your gut feelings," Fiona looked around the room. "So, if the relic wasn't in the display, where did he put it?"

"It would have to be somewhere in the building that a lot of people didn't know about. A secret hiding place," Celeste said.

"Probably not on the main floor." Morgan lowered her voice so the new visitors who had wandered into the room couldn't hear her. "I wonder if we can slip into the basement or attic to search."

Celeste leaned back to look out into the lobby. "That could get tricky. We might have to come up with some sort of story for Bernadette."

"Maybe we won't have to." Jolene looked up from her smartphone where she'd been typing. "I think that if whoever broke in was looking for the relic, they got confused about the clues. The pattern on the obelisk matches the pattern on the cement on the corners of this building, right?"

"Right. That's why we're *in* the building." Fiona said. "Because Ezra hid the relic in here, or at least that's what he implied."

"Not *in* here," Jolene said. "Outside."

"Outside?" Celeste looked incredulous. "I'm sure someone would have noticed it just sitting around outside by now."

"Not if it were hidden in a secret compartment inside a cornerstone." Jolene held the phone out for them to look at the screen. "Cornerstones are common in buildings and some of them have been used as time capsules. This building was built in Ezra's day ... maybe he had something to do with the construction and made a secret compartment."

The screen showed the corner of a building with small concrete slabs like those on the Oblate Museum. One of the slabs was slid open, revealing a small compartment inside. "This building has similar construction. It could have one of these."

Morgan was already halfway to the door. "Let's check it out."

The concrete and brick construction was unusual for an old, New England grange hall, which were typically built from wood. Fiona couldn't help but wonder if maybe Ezra did have something to do with its construction and chose the materials and style on purpose so he could have a place to stash the relic.

"I think it would be one of the bottom corners," Jolene said as they walked slowly around the building. She bent down to touch one of them, pressing and pulling. The piece didn't budge. "I'm not sure if one can just open them by pressing. It seems like that would be too easy."

"Right, but what other option do we have? Let's check out all four corners and see if Morgan gets a vibe," Celeste said.

"No pressure there." Morgan rolled her eyes and the others laughed, but she continued around the building to the back and focused her attention on the corners of the building.

The back was a small alley-like area with another building behind it—which was good, because no one could see what they were doing. If they were about to retrieve an important paranormal relic, Fiona figured it was probably better if there were no witnesses.

She scooped up a few stones anyway, just in case. Not that her shotgun stones trick was working, but she figured it couldn't hurt.

Morgan homed in on the east corner. She bent down and touched the cornerstone with the tips of her fingers. She pressed, then pulled, then pried, but the stone did not budge.

She looked up at the others. "I think this might be it, but it seems to be stuck or sealed."

Jolene squinted at the stone, then fished in her pocketbook coming up with a pocket knife. She squatted beside Morgan and started prying at the corner of the stone. Fiona heard the sound of concrete scraping on concrete.

"It's coming. It just takes a little wiggling." Jolene pried at the edge of the stone and it slid back, revealing a dark, black hole.

"Holy heck." Celeste turned to Jolene. "You were right."

"Yeah, now let's see what's in there."

All four girls bent down to peer into the black hole. Fiona couldn't see a thing in there. The opening was about six inches wide by four inches tall, but since it was black inside, Fiona couldn't tell how far back it went. Jolene fiddled with her cell phone to activate the flashlight app, then aimed it into the hole.

Fiona's stomach sank. "It's empty."

"Wait a minute." Jolene stuck her arm inside up to the elbow, twisting this way and that to feel all around the inside. Her eyes narrowed and her face scrunched.

"There's something, but I can't quite grab it ... got it!" A look of triumph spread across Jolene's face as she slowly pulled her arm out, revealing her clenched fist.

The girls huddled around in a circle, watching as Jolene unclenched her fist to reveal ... a Black Crow licorice.

"What the heck?" Morgan said as they stared at the round confection.

Fiona was so focused on the candy in Jolene's hand that she hadn't paid attention to her surroundings. A scraping sound behind her caught her attention and she whirled around to see three large, bearded men.

"Well, well. What have you got there?" The largest gestured toward Jolene's hand which she quickly closed. "Don't bother hiding it from me, because you're going to hand it to me right now … or we'll kill you on the spot."

Chapter Seven

Fiona's heart froze. The three men were a lot bigger than her and her sisters. The largest one, the one who had spoken, sneered at them. To his left, a man with a red beard stood in a fighting stance, mirrored by another man with a black beard on his right.

"Okay. Here you go! Jolene's fingers flew open and she thrust her hand out at red-beard. A stream of black goo ringed in glowing orange poured out of her hand like molten lava and hit red-beard in the face.

Red-beard screamed. His hands flew up and he staggered backward just as black beard pulled a weird-looking rock out of his pocket and aimed it at Jolene.

"Jo, Lookout!" Morgan tied to jump in between the rock and Jolene. The momentum caused her to crash into black beard. They tumbled to the ground and the rock smashed into a million pieces. Each of the pieces glowed a bright white, giving the appearance of a string of Christmas lights piled on the ground. Their glow winked out and the rocks disappeared. Black beard threw Morgan off and she stumbled backward, her shoulders slumping as she fell to the ground.

"What the heck was tha—" Fiona didn't have time to finish her sentence. Large-beard threw a glowing, white rope toward her and she had to duck out of the way to keep from getting hit. She watched in horror as the rope hit the ground, sparks flew in the air and she hopped around to avoid them.

Beside her, Jolene hopped around, too. Her wounded hand was cradled against her chest, her face contorted in pain. Morgan was coming awake in the corner, but still looked dazed.

Out of the corner of her eye, Fiona saw Celeste gearing up for one of her karate moves. She shot her leg up, her heel connecting with black beard's jaw.

Were they winning or losing?

Fiona had no idea. She could see that red-beard was out of commission with the black goo, black beard was busy fighting off Celeste, but Morgan was slumped in a stupor and large-beard was advancing on her and Jolene.

Fiona's heart pounded in her chest, since Jolene was still holding her hand in pain—it was up to her to fight off large-beard. She tightened her fist against the rocks she'd picked up earlier and focused her energy on them with all her might. She thought back to what her father had always told her when she was a little girl—if you wanted something bad enough, you could make it happen if you *believed*.

But did she believe?

As a child, it seemed so simple. But now as an adult, sometimes she felt like all that magical belief had disappeared. She didn't have much of a choice right now, though, so she flung the rocks at large-beard and jumped back.

Fiona felt a glimmer of triumph as an ember of red glow surrounded the rocks. They hit large-beard in the chest, bounced off and fell to the ground, leaving small burn marks in his blue nylon jacket. Too bad it wasn't enough to stop him. He merely looked down at the rocks, then back at Fiona.

"Is that all you got?" He laughed as he lunged toward her, the rope in his hand. She backed up until the cold bricks of the wall stopped her. He raised the rope as if to slip it around her neck. She squeezed her eyes shut.

"Leave her alone!" Jolene yelled. Fiona opened her eyes in time to see a purple ball of energy sear large-beard's forehead. He staggered backward, bumping into black beard, who had just been kicked in the jaw by Celeste for the second time.

Jolene didn't wait for them to recover. She thrust her fingers out, pummeling all three men with tiny energy balls.

"Retreat!" large-beard yelled. The other two didn't need any encouragement. They had already turned and were running back down the alley.

Celeste rushed to Morgan, helping her up.

"Are you okay?" Jolene asked Fiona.

"Yes," Fiona answered. She was fine physically, but mentally she felt like crap. Her stupid rocks hadn't worked and she hadn't been able to do anything to defend herself or her sisters. Instead, she'd had to depend on Jolene, who was already injured. The other sisters all had defensive skills. Fiona felt like a boat anchor.

"Are *you* okay?" she asked, indicating Jolene's hand.

"I'm fine." Jolene held her hand up. "It's just a little burn from the melted licorice. You can fix that up right away with one of your carnelian healing stones."

That cheered Fiona up. Maybe she couldn't help fight off bad guys, but in the past, her carnelian stones had been able to speed up healing dramatically. At least she could help out with the aftermath of a paranormal encounter.

"You guys okay?" Jolene and Fiona walked over to join Celeste, who was helping Morgan get steady on her feet.

"Yeah. What was that thing?" Morgan asked. "It felt like it drained all the energy out of me."

"I think that's one of those geodes that Bly used on me before." Jolene glanced down at the ground to make sure all the pieces were gone. "That's exactly what it does."

"I'm glad he didn't get a chance to use it on all of us," Celeste said. "Who knows what might have happened if we were all incapacitated."

"Yeah," Jolene frowned. "I guess they wanted something that was in that cornerstone, but I'm pretty sure it wasn't the licorice."

"Good point. What *were* they after?" Celeste asked.

"My guess is they were after the relic," Morgan answered. "Which they thought was in the cornerstone."

Fiona's brow creased. "But the cornerstone was empty."

"Right," Morgan said. "Which brings up the question ... if the attackers were Bly's guys and they didn't know the cornerstone was empty, then who took the relic?"

Chapter Eight

"It's simple." Jolene slipped a k-cup into the coffee machine, then turned and leaned her backside against the counter. "The licorice killer must have taken the relic."

Morgan pressed her lips together. "But why would he leave a licorice in the cornerstone?"

Celeste backed out of the fridge with an armful of leafy greens and headed toward the juicer. "Maybe he was taunting us."

"*Mew.*" Belladonna appeared in the doorway to the butler's pantry, and rubbed the side of her face against the corner of the door jamb before snaking her paw under the cabinet and batting a small object across the kitchen floor.

"But if the licorice killer took the relic, then who broke into the museum?" Johanna asked, her eyes tracking the object as it skittered in front of her, then disappeared under the lip of the cabinet near the sink.

"Maybe there are two different parties looking for the relic," Morgan suggested. "One group broke into the museum and the other—the licorice killer—got into the cornerstone."

"That would make sense." Celeste pulled spinach out of a bag and piled it into a bowl already loaded with wheat grass and kale. "Maybe the bearded guys were the ones that broke in.

They realized the relic wasn't among any of the items they stole, but they found a clue to look in the cornerstone and came back only to discover us looking in there first."

"That's an interesting theory." Morgan tapped a fingernail against her coffee mug. "But don't you guys think it's strange that they took several items? I mean, why not just take one item—the relic?"

Jolene took her full coffee mug to the island and slid into one of the stools. "It's obvious. They don't know what the relic is, so they took everything they thought *might* be the relic."

Johanna nodded. "That could very well be. After all, we don't know what it is, either."

"*Merow*!" Belladonna scooted across the room and swiped her paw under the cabinet near the sink, extracting the object and batting it over toward the back door like a hockey player testing out his slap shot.

Jolene watched the object shoot past her, a smile quirking her lips. Belladonna frequently amused herself by batting and chasing little items, like plastic milk bottle caps and elastic bands, and she was a lot of fun to watch.

But Jolene was only momentarily distracted by the cat's antics. She brought her attention back to the problem at hand, pressing her lips together as she considered their conversation. "If what you guys are saying is true, then the licorice killer and the beards are racing against each other—and us—for the relic."

"Right, but we don't know if the licorice killer is one of Bly's guys, or if he *killed* one of Bly's guys," Fiona said.

"This licorice killer person scares me. He must be very powerful to take out one of Bly's minions." Celeste loaded some greens into the tunnel of the juicer and switched it on. The noise made it impossible to talk, so Jolene thought about the facts of the case while the machine made its headache-inducing noise.

So far, all they really knew was that Ezra Finch had hidden an important relic decades ago. That relic was infused with energy from an energy master, which could be disastrous if it fell into the wrong hands. One or more groups of paranormal bad guys were after the relic, one of whom had a penchant for Black Crow licorices and had already killed at least one person. They had no idea what the relic was or where to look next.

Mercifully, the whirring of the juicer stopped and Jolene watched Celeste pour the green, gloppy liquid into a glass. "So, it looks like we're up against both the licorice killer *and* Bly's guys. But who has the relic?"

"The licorice killer must have it, since it was no longer in the cornerstone," Morgan said.

Johanna's left brow rose a fraction of an inch. "*If* it was in there in the first place."

Fiona nodded. "That's right. We only know that the licorice killer was in there before us. We don't know he actually found anything."

"And if the bearded attackers reported back that we were in the cornerstone, than Bly probably thinks *we* have it and he'll be coming after us," Celeste said over the rim of her juice glass.

"*Breeeow!*" Belladonna's paw shot out at lightning speed, sending the object zipping across the floor. Jolene frowned as she watched it. It didn't look like a milk carton ring or any of Belladonna's usual toys. She stuck her foot out to intercept it. The object bounced off her foot, then spun to a stop an inch away. It was an old, brown cork. She slid off her stool and grabbed it off the floor then stood, holding it up in front of her face. "What is this? I'm not sure Belladonna should be playing with it."

"*Brrrrrowgh.*" Belladonna glared at Jolene as if to say that she was perfectly capable of figuring out what was safe to play with on her own.

Morgan squinted at the cork. "That looks like one of my remedy bottle corks." She held her hand out and Jolene dropped the cork into her palm. "Yep. It's okay. My remedies are all natural."

Jolene narrowed her eyes. "But don't you use antique bottles. What if the cork still has some old poison on it?"

Morgan closed the cork in her fist and put her hands on her hips. "I sanitize the bottles and the corks, of course. You don't think I'd be giving remedies to people in bottles with poisonous corks, do you? But anyway, I have no idea how she got this. I don't leave my stuff lying around. I just thought she was batting around some balled-up masking tape."

"Me, too." Jolene felt bad that she'd thought the cork might not be sanitized. She knew Morgan was diligent about safety with her remedies. Still, it unnerved her that the cat was batting around the cork and she hadn't noticed what it was. Which made her wonder what other items the cat played with that she assumed was one thing when it was really something else. Assumptions were too easy to make, and Jolene knew from her private investigator training that assuming was never a good idea.

And *that* thought made her wonder if they were making too many assumptions about the relic and the parties involved. "I'm not sure what to think about this. We can't assume anything about Bly and the licorice killer, or even that they are the only two groups after the relic."

Celeste said, "Sheesh, how many people do you think are looking for the darn thing?"

"The amount of people looking for the relic isn't what worries me the most," Morgan said. "What worries me the most is who *has* it now."

"Nobody has it." A voice shot in from the hallway shortly seconds before its owner, a tall, sharply-dressed woman appeared in the doorway. Jolene recognized the woman as Dorian Hall, Luke's mysterious boss. Dorian was decked out in her usual, all-black office attire outfit. Her short, black hair was salted with a few grays, but her dark eyes were sharp and clear.

"How did you get in here?" Morgan leaned back in her chair to look down the hall toward the front door.

Dorian looked back over her shoulder. "Luke said you girls always leave the door open. I knocked but no one answered, so I just walked in."

Jolene frowned at her. Luke was always on them about the security at the house, and with good reason. Jolene wasn't sure she wanted everyone walking right in ... not even Dorian. Belladonna must have felt the same way because she arched her back and hissed at the tall woman, then slinked her way out of the room, giving Dorian a wide berth as she passed her in the doorway.

"Whats with her?" Dorian watched the cat sidestep down the hallway.

"Maybe she doesn't like people walking in," Fiona said. "And how do you know no one has the relic?"

"We have our ways." Dorian crossed her arms on her chest and leaned her shoulder on the doorframe. "Anyway, we have word there is more than one group after the relic, but no one has it in their possession yet."

"Just what *is* it?" Celeste asked.

"That, I can't tell you."

Morgan narrowed her eyes at Dorian. "Really? You seem to know everything else."

Dorian pushed off the doorframe and stepped over to the kitchen island. Leaning her palms on the surface, she bent forward slightly and fixed the girls with an earnest look. "Our outfit can only recover so much information. We have limited resources. That's why we need you girls to step it up and get the relic before Bly does."

"So, you're hiring us?" Johanna looked shrewdly at Dorian. Dorian's company, which the girls knew was really a secret branch of the government despite her denials, had hired them to do a couple of other jobs and they paid well. Of course, the Blackmoores didn't really need money. Not since they'd discovered a priceless hoard of treasure hidden by the ancestor, Isaiah

Blackmoore. But since Johanna's return, she'd been running their activities like a finely honed business and she didn't think it was wise to turn down money. Jolene agreed with her philosophy—you never knew when earnings might dry up.

"Yes, I already have Luke out trying to identify the other groups looking for the relic." Dorian surveyed the room. "Have you girls had any interaction with any other paranormal groups?"

The sisters looked at each other. The girls had learned that the less information they gave out, the better. Jolene knew each of them was wondering if they should tell Dorian. But know that they were working for her, Jolene figured they should probably come clean. After all, they *were* on the same side and Dorian might have information or resources that could help them.

Johanna must have thought the same thing. She looked at Dorian out of the corner of her eye. "As a matter of fact, we have. My girls have already been followed *and* attacked, so we can't accept your usual rate. This job is much more dangerous."

"Already attacked? You're already looking into it, then? I figured you would be." A smug smile spread across Dorian's face. "And you were doing that for free."

Johanna shrugged. "That's right. So you owe us. I figure a ten percent increase should cover it."

Dorian frowned. "I don't know if my bosses will agree to that."

Johanna's left brow ticked up. "Well, then maybe we'll recover the relic and use it for ourselves instead of handing it over to you…"

Dorian held her palms up. "Okay, ten percent, but not a penny more. And the next job goes back to the regular rate."

Johanna stared at Dorian for a few seconds then stuck out her hand. "Okay. Deal."

The two women shook hands, then Dorian said, "Tell me about the attack."

The girls related the events of the day, including the person following them at the Finch farm and the attack behind the museum.

Dorian's face turned thoughtful as she tapped a red-tipped fingernail on her pursed lips. "So, there *is* more than one party."

"Yes, but *who* is the other party?" Morgan asked.

"I'm not sure, but I did hear that your old friend Overton has made some friends who possess very interesting paranormal gifts."

"*Sheriff* Overton?" Morgan's eyes widened. Sheriff Overton had been a thorn in the girls' side since Johanna disappeared. He'd originally come to town to investigate her supposed death and ended up harassing the girls any chance he got.

What they'd never realized was that he was one of the 'bad guys'.

Overton had left town mysteriously two years earlier, but the girls had been unfortunate enough to have a recent run-in with him where they'd been forced to barter a meteorite locket that enhanced paranormal abilities for their freedom. If Overton had paranormal associates that were using the locket, there was no telling what he might be up to.

"Do you think he's after the relic?" Fiona asked.

Dorian shrugged. "It's possible, although he seems to be more interested in money than old relics. But if he thinks it will put him in a position of power, then he might want it."

"Great, now we have to watch out for him, too," Jolene muttered.

"True, but he's no match for us," Celeste said.

"I'd be more worried about his associate," Johanna said.

"We don't know for sure that Overton is the other person after the relic." Morgan turned to Dorian. "Any idea who else would be after it?"

"I don't know. A rogue paranormal, perhaps?" Dorian suggested.

"Do you have anyone in your rogues' gallery that has a fetish for Black Crow licorice?" Jolene asked.

"Excuse me?"

"We found Black Crow licorice near the body and in the cornerstone. And on the road where the person that was following us had been parked."

"Interesting." Dorian shook her head. "But I don't know of any paranormal that likes licorice. Maybe they are from a new faction we have yet to identify."

"That's a big help." Jolene blurted the words out and was rewarded with a sharp scowl from Dorian.

"So, what do we do now?" Celeste asked, ignoring the adversarial undercurrent between Jolene and Dorian.

Dorian glanced at the slim watch on her wrist. "That's up to you girls. I gotta run." She headed out of the kitchen, her heels emitting a staccato clack on the black and white tile floor.

"Don't forget to send the first payment," Johanna yelled after her.

"Payment for what?" Mateo appeared in the doorway, loaded up with grocery bags.

"Cripes. This place is like Grand Central Station." Jolene stared at Mateo. "What are you doing back here again? I thought you left."

Mateo slid the bags onto the counter next to the fridge. "I'm just loading up for Thanksgiving."

"Thanksgiving?" Fiona frowned. "We don't usually do anything for Thanksgiving since Mom die ... err ... disappeared."

"Yeah, and now she's back, so you girls have a big reason to be thankful." Mateo started unloading the bags onto the counter.

"Yeah, I guess you're right." Morgan smiled at Johanna, then got up to help Mateo put the groceries in the fridge. "But where have you been?"

Mateo bent down, his head in the fridge as he put potatoes into the vegetable crisper. His voice came out muffled. "Out and about."

"We were attacked, you know," Jolene blurted out. Then grimaced, thinking the statement sounded stupid and wondering why she'd even said it.

Mateo backed out of the fridge and winked at her. "You can take care of yourselves. I can see none of you are hurt."

Jolene bristled. She wondered why it bothered her so much that Mateo hadn't been there to come to their rescue. The girls had fought off bad guys without him plenty of times, so why did his absence bother her now?

"Anyway, what was Dorian doing here?" Mateo opened a kitchen cabinet, frowned at the contents and then opened the one next to it.

"She hired us to look for the relic," Fiona said.

"Uh-huh." Mateo shoved a can of cream of mushroom soup in the cabinet. "You guys should really clean these cabinets out. They're so cluttered, I don't know how you can find anything."

Jolene rolled her eyes behind his back and Celeste snickered.

"So, where have you been?" Morgan asked. "Did your absence have anything to do with the relic?"

"Not really. I was on a recon mission to see what Bly was up to. He definitely has plans for the relic, so we'd better find it soon. It worries me that there are other groups involved. I can't help but feel something isn't as it seems."

Morgan pressed her lips together. "You know, I get the same feeling."

"So, I guess the cornerstone must have been empty," Celeste said. "But all three of the groups were looking in there, so was the relic ever in there or did we all follow the wrong clue?"

"Good question," Morgan said.

"So, *now* what do we do?" Fiona echoed Celeste's earlier question.

Jolene puffed out her cheeks. "I guess we need to keep looking for the relic. We need to revisit the clues."

"It would be a lot easier to find the darn thing if we knew what it was," Morgan said.

Johann nodded. "Uh huh. Or who the players were."

"The break-in at the museum must be related somehow and I'm pretty sure that boat I saw has something to do with this," Celeste said.

"Right." Fiona whipped out her cell and started texting. "Where is Jake? He was supposed to look into that."

"I say we regroup tonight when Luke and Jake are here. We can map out a plan, figure out what to do next and then start fresh tomorrow," Morgan suggested.

"Yes, but bright and early. I'm sure Bly and the other bad guys are working well into the night to find the relic," Celeste said.

Johanna's face turned grim. "One thing's for sure. Whatever the relic is, you can bet Bly has an evil plan for it."

Mateo pushed a can of fried onion rings into one of the cabinets, shut the door and turned around to face them. "I'm sure you're right about Bly. What worries me more is that the *other* guy might be planning something even worse."

Chapter Nine

Jolene looked over the top of her laptop screen at her sisters and their boyfriends, who were settling in on the overstuffed couches and chairs in the east sitting room. Jolene was just starting to do some research on the mysterious boat Celeste had seen in the cove when Johanna, who had insisted on cleaning up the dinner dishes on her own, finally wheeled herself in.

"Did Mateo leave?" Celeste's brows mashed together over the rim of her tea cup.

Johanna nodded. "Yes. He had to go off again, but he said he'd be back in a few days."

"That guy sure is mysterious." Jake's brows ticked up over his steely, gray eyes.

"Yeah, are you really sure we can trust him?" Cal Reed, Celeste's boyfriend and longtime friend of the family asked. Cal had grown up in Noquitt and the Blackmoore sisters had known him since they were little. He was almost like a brother to all of them, but he and Celeste had been particularly close—best friends on a platonic level until the year before, when they'd become more than friends. Jolene smiled at the thought. Cal was a great guy, and she'd always thought he and Celeste were perfect for each other. It was about time the two of them figured out what the whole family had known all along.

Johanna shot Cal a look.

"Of course we can. If it wasn't for Mateo, we might not have made it out of Fury Rock alive. You know that," Johanna said, referring to the harrowing events earlier in the year at the secret underground laboratory of Dr. Mortimer Bly—an evil paranormal whose face to the world was that of a scientist searching for alternative energy.

Cal tilted his head in submission. "Yeah, that's true. He just seems kind of … elusive."

"It's part of his charm." Johanna smiled and slid her eyes to Jolene.

Jolene chose to ignore her mother and focus on the task at hand. Her fingers flew over the keyboard.

She was usually pretty good at hacking into online databases. Computer forensics was her forte and while she usually tried to do things within the law, there were times when she had to step over the line. Too bad the Perkins Cove harbor didn't keep information online. All they had to go by was the boat registration number, which didn't seem to come up in any of the state databases.

"Did you find out anything about that boat?" she asked Jake. Jake had hired Jolene earlier in the year to help with his private investigator business. His forte was getting information from people and Jolene knew he'd spent most of the day talking to his various contacts at the cove and around town. The two of them had complementary skills sets and worked great together, although Jolene thought Jake could be a little overprotective of her at times—kind of like an unwanted big brother. She was working on that, but she had to admit that sometimes it did feel kind of nice to have someone watching out for her ... as long as it didn't cramp her style.

Jake twisted his lips. "I did find out something, but I don't think it helps us much. The boat is registered to a shell company. I can't track who the owner is."

"What's the name of it?" Luke asked.

"*Light of Day Ventures.*"

"Could that be a front for Bly?" Luke reached over to help Johanna, who was trying to maneuver the chair so she could transfer herself onto one of the armchairs.

Johanna pushed him away, her face serious with determination. "I can do it myself."

Jolene watched her mother with amusement. She'd only been fourteen when her mother had disappeared and she hadn't gotten to know her well as an adult. But now, she realized the woman was a dynamo of determination and grit.

"*Light of Day Ventures...*" Morgan narrowed her eyes thoughtfully as Johanna lifted herself out of the chair, her legs shaking slightly as she stepped sideways and plopped down in the armchair.

"It could be," Johanna said after she was settled. "Sounds like something he might use. The word 'light' could be a reference to energy."

"Well, we already know he has people here in town. I mean, assuming the bearded Neanderthals that attacked us are with Bly," Fiona said.

"Speaking of that attack..." Luke's face turned serious. "I think we'd better tighten up security here at the house. It's no secret that Bly knows you live here, and clearly there's a battle going on for this relic so he'll probably have his minions break in sooner or later."

Jolene and Morgan rolled their eyes. They knew that tightening up security meant Luke would have men watching the house and probably tailing them. Even though they'd installed a high-tech security system at his insistence, just months ago, Luke didn't skimp when it came to their safety. To the girls, it felt like a restriction on their freedom. None of them thought they needed Luke's protection, but they'd learned early on that it was a waste of time arguing with him.

"Do what you must." Morgan smiled at him affectionately, then turned to Fiona. "But he has a point. We should make sure we are protected.

How are you coming with those obsidian amulets?"

Fiona had made protective amulets for them out of a black stone called obsidian earlier in the year. Before they'd been forced to give the meteorite locket to Overton, Fiona had boosted the power of several obsidian stones with the locket and made amulets for each of them. The amulets had the power to deflect negative energy, but they'd been damaged in a fight with Bly's minions. Fiona had already drained the bad energy they'd absorbed by burying them in the earth for several weeks. She was in the middle of doing the rest of the repairs at *Sticks and Stones,* the shop that she and Morgan owned together.

"With all this excitement, I almost forgot about them," Fiona said. "But I'm almost done. Maybe we can stop over and I can finish them after we visit Thaddeus."

"Let's plan on it," Morgan replied.

Jolene shut the laptop. She hadn't found anything more on the boat than Jake had. "So all we really know is that one or more other parties are after the relic."

"It must be more than one, because someone was killed, so there's got to be at least two other groups," Celeste said.

"Did you find out anything more about the victim?" Johanna asked. "Is he related to that archaeologist that Cal knows?"

"I looked into that," Cal said. "But Gunner Swain is very private. He keeps his family life close to the vest and there's nothing on his siblings. I don't really know him, either. I just know *of* him."

"And what do you know of him?" Johanna asked. "Is there a reason he would be involved in looking for the relic?"

Cal pressed his lips together. "I doubt it. As far as I know he's not involved in any paranormal stuff. He's made a lot of really great finds. Mostly Egyptian, Mayan and Aztec. He's quite wealthy. I don't see why he would have anything to do with it unless there is an important archeological find related to it."

Jolene raised a brow at her sisters. They were all thinking the same thing ... there *was* an important find right below their house. Except Swain couldn't have known that—no one except them knew.

"Let's set that aside for now and talk about the groups that we do know are involved," Luke said.

Jolene nodded. "Good idea. There must be at least two groups, and one of them broke into the museum so they must have thought it was a clue just like we did."

"The break-in could have been a coincidence," Fiona said. "Kids or vandals, like Bernadette said."

Morgan scrunched up her face. "No way. That would be too much of a coincidence. Besides, kids don't steal old apothecary jars. That stuff has no value."

"Right," Jake agreed. "I don't know of any meth lab that uses old chemistry equipment, despite Bernadette's theory."

"But why would whoever was looking for the relic take them?" Fiona asked.

"We need to see a list of all the items that were taken." Jolene opened the laptop again. "Maybe I can look in the police database or someone can sweet-talk that information out of Brody. It's possible they just grabbed whatever they could, *or* they took all the items to camouflage the one they were really after."

"So no one would guess what the relic really is?" Celeste asked.

Jolene nodded as she tapped on the keyboard.

"Do you girls think the people that attacked you are the same ones who broke in?" Jake asked.

"We're not sure," Morgan replied. "It doesn't seem likely that they would come back so soon."

"Unless they found something in the items they took that pointed to the cornerstone," Fiona added.

"We know whoever attacked us wasn't with the licorice killer because he'd already been to the cornerstone," Fiona said.

"So, that means either the licorice killer broke in, or there are three groups after the darn thing," Luke pointed out.

"Good point," Johanna said. "But I wonder *how* the licorice killer knew to look in the cornerstone in the first place?"

"He was at the Finch farm and saw us in the graveyard, so he probably just followed the same clue that we did," Jolene said as she perused the information in the Noquitt Police database she'd just gained unauthorized access to.

"Which apparently was wrong," Celeste pointed out.

"But it does explain why that cornerstone slid out so easily. He'd already pried it open so the cement wasn't even holding it in." Morgan pressed her lips together. "But what if someone was in there *before* the licorice killer?"

"Yeah, like the people posing as Thaddeus Finch's nephews," Jolene said. "They were at the nursing home right before us, so they could have been following the same clue trail."

"And *they* might have the relic," Fiona added.

Celeste shook her head. "No, Dorian said that no one has it yet. It's still up for grabs."

"Right." Jolene slammed the laptop shut. "The official list of the stolen museum items isn't posted yet, so we have to go with the facts we have available to us right now."

"Which are?" Fiona prompted.

The girls looked at each other for a few seconds, then Morgan spoke. "All signs indicate that we got the clue wrong in the first place, but I still feel like the clue lies in the graveyard."

"Maybe we misinterpreted what Ezra said," Jolene suggested.

Fiona turned to Celeste. "What exactly did he say?"

Celeste squeezed her eyes shut, trying to remember. "He said he provided a clue before he left this world and that it was 'in the center', which he said was the 'most important part of the graveyard'." Celeste opened her sky-blue eyes. "Then he went off to play poker with some of the other ghosts."

"Poker?" Jake fixed her with a bemused look. He was still getting used to the fact that the girls had paranormal gifts, especially Celeste's ability to talk to ghosts.

Celeste laughed. "Yeah, I guess ghosts still play cards."

Fiona spread her arms out. "Well, that's exactly where we went. To the center of the graveyard—the obelisk."

"Maybe we interpreted the clue wrong, though," Jolene said. "Maybe it didn't have anything to do with the museum."

"But the other people searching for the relic went there, too," Celeste pointed out.

"Maybe *they* also interpreted the clue wrong," Jolene answered.

Fiona sighed. "So we're back to square one."

"Not quite," Morgan said. "But I do think we need to retrace our steps and see if we can figure things from a different angle."

"It might be a good idea to get clarification on what *exactly* Ezra meant," Johanna said.

Celeste made a face. "He was really vague. I don't know if he'll be more specific or even if I'd be able to see him if we went back to the graveyard. Unfortunately, I can't conjure ghosts up at will."

"No, but there might be someone else who can give you some insight as to where he was coming from and that might help you figure out what he meant," Johanna said.

"Who?"

"His great-grandson, Thaddeus Finch."

Chapter Ten

"Thaddeus Finch is senile. I don't see how he can help us figure out what Ezra really meant. And even if he gives us info, can we trust it?" Jolene asked as they head into the lobby of the *Fiddlers Rest Nursing Home* the next morning.

"Mom seems to think it will help, so what the heck." Morgan shrugged. "Besides, we don't have anything else to try."

They stepped up to the nurses' station. The same woman who had been there the previous day looked up at them, a flicker of recognition passing across her face. "Are you girls here to see Mr. Finch again?"

"Yes," they chorused.

"Well, head on down. You remember where it is?"

"Yep. Thanks."

Thaddeus Finch was sitting in the same recliner in the corner, with the same orange and green afghan on his lap. The aide, Wendy, was standing beside him with the television remote.

"Do you want to watch *Wheel of Fortune*?" Wendy was asking as Morgan tapped on the door lightly.

Thaddeus looked over at the door with cloudy eyes. A smile spread across his face as he focused on the sisters standing in the doorway.

"Well, well. Come on in." He straightened in his chair and motioned with his hand for them to enter. He squinted up at them. "Say, aren't you the Blackmoore girls?"

Jolene smiled. *Maybe he's lucid today.* "Yes, we are."

"Did you get what you were looking for out at the farm?" His face turned wistful. "How is the farm coming along? I sure do wish I could go back there."

"It's very nice," Jolene lied. No sense in telling him it had gone to ruin.

Morgan nodded. "In fact, we liked it so much we have some more questions about your great-granddaddy."

"Ezra?" Finch chuckled. "Now, he was a character. 'Course I don't remember much about him. I was just a wee lad when he passed on. But I do remember that he had a lot of confidence."

"I heard he was a famous pharmacist," Morgan said.

"Yes, that's right. I'm afraid the fame might have gone to his head. I always remember him saying how important he was. And he loved his pharmacy, 'course it burned down now seven years ago." Finch screwed up has face and looked up at the ceiling. "Or was it longer? I don't know, but it was very upsetting. He had a bunch of special equipment. Bottles and those grinding stones. I was fascinated with them as a boy, but he wouldn't let me play with them."

"You must have been very close," Fiona said.

"Well, I reckon so. Never thought of it that way. He was mostly busy in the pharmacy, but he always cut out some time for me. You see, his wife Lila-Mae passed before I was born and he was right sick about it. Pappy said he went into a depression and threw himself into pharmacy work. That's when he got famous, I guess." Finch waved his hands. "I didn't pay much attention to that stuff. I was just a little kid, but I know he told me some of the light went out when Lila-Mae passed. He said marrying her was the happiest day of his life ... well, aside from the day he got that big pharmacy award. But anyway, I don't reckon you girls come here to hear an old man talk about the past."

"Actually, we did," Celeste said. "We'd love to know more about Ezra. What was he like? What did he like to do? What was important to him?"

"Well, I don't remember much, 'cept him talking about the pharmacy and Lila-Mae sometimes. He said she had the most curious, gray eyes." Finch thrust his thumb over his shoulder in the direction of Wendy, who had made herself almost invisible over by his bedside table. "Like my girl, Wendy, here."

Wendy smiled selfconsciously and Morgan noticed she did have unusual gray eyes, which complemented her hair nicely.

"They must have been very much in love," Morgan said.

"I suppose so. I don't know anything about love. Never married, myself." Finch paused, lost in thought. "I don't remember Ezra doing much else 'cept his pharmacy work, but he did like to play cards from time to time."

Jolene remembered Celeste had said his ghost had wandered off to play cards. "Was card playing important to him?"

"Nah. Not really. Oh, he liked it, but after his wife died, his true love was that pharmacy and his medicines."

"Do you know much about his pharmacy business?" Morgan asked.

"Nah, I was a kid. Didn't pay much attention to business. But I loved the old coot. Him, my granddaddy, and my pappy. All gone now." His eyes shone and he leaned forward in the chair. "But I done them right. Buried them in the family graveyard and kept the graves neat and tidy. I even put up that obelisk right near Ezra - he always said he was the most important part of the family, so I figure it should be near him."

Morgan narrowed her eyes at Finch. "Did you say *you* put the obelisk in the graveyard after Ezra died?"

Why, yes. I figured it was a nice memorial for the graveyard. 'Course I kept it nice and all. Tended the graves regularly and was even hoping that someday I might be laid to rest—"

"That's it!" Morgan snapped her fingers, cutting Finch off in mid-sentence. She spun on her heels and headed toward the door, motioning for the others to follow. When they got out into the hall, she turned and poked her head back in the door. "Thanks, Mr. Finch, it's been great talking to you, but we gotta run!"

***

"If the obelisk wasn't even *in* the graveyard during Ezra's time, then the similarities between the pattern on the obelisk and the Oblate Museum must just be a coincidence. It can't be the clue that Ezra's ghost said he left ... the real clue must be on his grave." Morgan explained, her words coming out in short puffs of condensation as they picked their way through the tall grass on the Finch farm toward the graveyard.

"That makes perfect sense," Celeste agreed. "Thaddeus said that Ezra thought he was pretty important, and his ghost told me he left the clue in 'the center—the most important part of the graveyard'. I thought he was talking about the obelisk, but now it makes sense that he would be talking about his own gravestone."

Jolene scrunched her face up. "Seriously? How could a guy leave a clue on his own grave?"

"That is what we need to find out," Morgan said. They walked up the cement steps to the family plot. A chill crept up her spine and she stopped and turned, looking back out over the field behind them.

"Are we being followed again?" Fiona asked.

"Possibly. Probably." Morgan gazed out over the field, her eyes searching for any movement that would indicate they were being followed while her intuition focused on locating a presence her eyes couldn't see.

Was someone out there?

She felt something wasn't right, but couldn't see anyone. She took a deep breath of crisp, cold air. It was heavy with the wet, frosty smell of snow. A glance up at the gray sky told her the first flakes would come any minute. She turned her attention back to the graveyard. "Let's just focus on the task at hand and keep our eyes peeled for visitors."

They approached the old, slate stone that marked the grave of Ezra Finch. It wasn't anything extraordinary—tall, with a rounded tombstone top and a weeping willow engraved on it.

As they stood there looking down at it, the snow started. Big, fat flakes landed silently on their jackets. One fluttered onto Morgan's eyelashes, obstructing her view, and she brushed it away.

Jolene squatted in front of the gravestone.

"Maybe this stone has a hidden compartment in it, like the one we found out west," she said, referring to an old gravestone on another of their missions that had a secret housed in a slide-out piece at the base.

"It would be a perfect place to hide a clue." Fiona wrapped her purple scarf around her neck. The snowflakes, which were falling faster now, stuck to her red hair like confetti.

Jolene pushed at the bottom of the stone, trying each of the four corners. "It doesn't seem like this one has a compartment."

Morgan was only half-paying attention. Something to the east caught her eye. The visibility was slowly being cut down by the storm, so it wasn't something she could see, but more something she could feel.

"What is it?" Jolene looked back over her shoulder in the direction of Morgan's gaze.

"I don't know. I think I'm just jittery." The storm was closing in, causing white-out conditions. She could barely see twenty feet away. The gravestones took on an eerie cast as they faded into the white background. Anyone could be out there and they wouldn't see them until it was too late. "Maybe we should come back later."

Jolene stood and brushed the snow from her pants. "Maybe. I can't find the compartment and I don't see how Ezra could hide something in his own gravestone, anyway."

"Maybe he didn't hide it … maybe he left the clue right on the stone." Celeste brushed the snow off the face of the stone and pointed at the inscription.

Morgan shielded her eyes and squinted at the rock through the driving snow. The inscription was typical, with the names, birth and death dates of Ezra and Lila-Mae Finch.

Celeste stepped closer to the stone. Tapping her finger on the poem inscribed below the names, she read it out loud.

"When two become one, the healing's begun. In my favorite place under the sun. Look to the west, I can finally rest."

"So you think that's the clue?" Fiona asked.

"Hey, wait! It looks like there's more below." Jolene squatted down again and brushed the snow that had accumulated in front of the stone. Just under the inscription, Morgan could see another line at the very bottom, almost under the soil line.

"What's that say?" Celeste bent down to look at it.

"I can only see the tops of the letters. I can't make out what they actually are."

Morgan noticed the wind had picked up considerably and the visibility had faded to almost nothing. A tingling at the back of her neck told her danger was near.

Jolene dug furiously at the soil with her gloved finger. "The ground is frozen. I can't uncover the last line." She had to shout over the wind to be heard.

"Something's not right!" Morgan looked around at her sisters and saw her concern mirrored in their eyes. The wind whipped their hair around their faces as they glanced around uneasily.

Morgan's heart sank. She could barely see two feet in front of her. She wondered if they could even make it back to the car when the wind increased, picking up the snowflakes from the ground and whipping them around, creating blizzard conditions.

She shouted for her sisters, but the wind snatched the words out of her mouth. The only sound she could hear was the gusting of the wind. The snow—so soft and fluffy just minutes ago—stung her cheeks like shards of ice. She whirled around, totally disoriented, her heart thudding in her chest.

Feeling an evil presence near them, she stumbled backward, the wind pushing at her, causing her to topple over. She crashed to the ground, pain searing her right arm and hip. She struggled to get back up, but the wind was too strong. It pinned her to the ground.

Crack!

Morgan felt a sharp pain above her right ear. And then, there was nothing but darkness.

***

Morgan woke to a mouth full of snow and a splitting headache. Her right side was practically frozen solid and she realized she was lying on the ground. Then she remembered what had happened. Her eyes flew open, focusing on Jolene, who lay ten feet away under a large tree limb.

Morgan, herself, had some smaller branches on top of her, but she easily pushed them off and ran over to her sister. Relief spread through her as she noticed Fiona and Celeste sitting up and shaking snow off their coats. Not Jolene, though. She lay as still as death.

"Jo! Are you okay?" Morgan ripped off her gloves and knelt in the snow, pressing two fingers on Jolene's neck. Her heart squeezed at Jolene's ghostly, white cheeks, but she had a pulse and her eyelashes fluttered slightly.

"Jolene! Wake up!" Fiona and Celeste moved the tree limb and joined Morgan beside their younger sister.

Jolene's ice-blue eyes flickered open and looked around, unfocused. Worry gnawed at Morgan's gut as she watched her sister push up to a sitting position, her brow furrowed as she looked around at Morgan, Fiona and Celeste in confusion.

"What's going on?" Jolene asked.

"Good question," Celeste replied. "There was a storm and you got hit by a tree limb."

Jolene looked at the large limb Celeste indicated and then past Morgan. Morgan followed her gaze. The snow and wind had stopped, but the cemetery looked a mess. Glancing up, Morgan could see the white, raw wood where the large limb had sheared off from the big, old oak tree. Smaller branches lay strewn about. But that wasn't the most startling sight. The most startling site was Ezra Finch's gravestone. It lay smashed in a million jagged pieces. Now they'd never know what that last line was.

"Are you okay?" Morgan asked again as they helped Jolene to her feet.

"Yes, of course." Jolene made a face. "It takes a lot more than a little branch to hurt me."

Morgan raised her left brow at Fiona and Celeste. The fuzzy look in Jolene's eyes had cleared and she *seemed* fine, but Morgan didn't want to take any chances. Trouble was, Jolene was stubborn and probably wouldn't listen to them if they wanted her to see a doctor. Morgan tried anyway. "I think we'd better take you to the hospital and get you checked out."

"No. No. I'm fine." Jolene pushed her sisters away and took a step forward. She was a little wobbly, but not too bad. She turned in a slow circle, looking all around them, her forehead creasing in a wrinkle that got deeper and deeper the more she looked.

"What the heck are we doing in a graveyard?"

Chapter Eleven

"If you can't remember what we were doing at Finch's, then I think you need a doctor." Morgan looked across the kitchen island at Jolene's pale face and regretted letting her sister talk her into taking her home instead of to the hospital.

Johanna gave Jolene a motherly frown. "She's right. You could have a concussion."

"Concussion? What happened?" Jake stood in the kitchen doorway, his face a mask of concern.

"A tree limb fell on Jolene and knocked her out," Morgan explained.

Jake crossed the kitchen and stood in front of Jolene. He tilted her head up toward the light and pried her eyelid open.

"Ouch!" She pulled away, covering her eye with her hand. "What are you doing?"

"Checking your pupils. I used to be a cop, remember? I know a little bit about concussions," Jake said. "Are you feeling nauseous or dizzy? Any blurred vision, headache, forgetfulness?"

"No. No. And no," Jolene said.

"Well, you *did* forget why we were at the Finch farm," Celeste pointed out.

"I'm fine. I'm not going to the hospital," Jolene said.

"Her pupils look okay and she doesn't seem to have any other symptoms. I guess we just watch her and make sure she doesn't show any signs of concussion. We can't force her to go to the hospital if she's too stubborn to know what's good for her." He shrugged. "How did you guys make out on the farm, anyway? Did you find a new clue? And how did the tree branch fall?"

The three sisters filled Jake and Johanna in on the trip to the cemetery, the clue on the gravestone and the strange, windy snowstorm. Luckily, Luke came in at the beginning so they didn't have to repeat themselves. Jolene leaned against the counter, unusually silent, taking it all in.

"Do you think the strange storm was some kind of paranormal force?" Luke asked.

"Maybe." Morgan looked at her sisters and they nodded. "If a paranormal can control energy, then why not the energy of the wind?"

Luke nodded. "There're forces out there we can't even imagine. But is this wind person in cahoots with Bly?"

"Good question," Fiona said. "We don't know who it was or who they were in cahoots with."

"It sounds like the trip out to the farm was eventful, but did it give you guys have a new lead on the relic?" Jake asked.

Fiona nodded. "Obviously the clue couldn't have been on the obelisk, so we think it was the epitaph on Ezra's gravestone. There was a poem on there and we think it might be the clue."

"Too bad we never got to read the bottom line of it," Celeste added.

"Why not?" Luke asked.

"The stone must have settled over the years and the very bottom was under the ground line. We could just see the tops of the letters but not enough to tell what letter it was," Fiona explained.

"And the stone blew to smithereens in the wind storm," Celeste added.

Jake snorted. "That must have been some wind storm. I don't think wind can blow up a stone."

Luke nodded, his face turning serious. "That's right. Whoever caused that must have some power. I want you girls to be extra careful from here on in. I'll put more guys on detail watching you."

Morgan sighed. She would have argued, but she knew it was futile. Luke was serious about safety, especially when it came to her. Which did make her feel all warm and fuzzy inside, except for the part where someone followed her around. At least Luke's guys were inconspicuous—she hardly knew they were there most of the time.

"But why would Bly—or whoever—want to smash the gravestone?"

"Probably so no one else could figure out the clue," Celeste said.

"Then it must be really important," Luke said. "That bottom line could be the key to finding the relic."

Jake's right brow ticked up. "Maybe we could go back and piece it together?"

Celeste shook her head. "The pieces are too small."

Johanna pressed her lips together. "I bet Cal could figure it out if you girls could draw the tops of the letters."

Morgan thought about that. Cal, an antique dealer by trade, loved history and one of his specialties was codes and encryption. He'd figured things out for them before. Too bad she couldn't remember what the bottom of the stone looked like. "I don't remember exactly what it looked like."

"That's okay. We have a secret weapon that can help us even if the bad guys destroyed the clue." Jake looked at Jolene. "Put your photographic memory to use and draw out what the top of that line looked like."

A look of panic crossed Jolene's face. "I can't. I don't remember."

Morgan's stomach sank. Was Jolene's memory gone for good? Hopefully not. But right now, they needed it. She glanced at her sisters and she could tell they were all thinking the same thing. What other unique skills had Jolene lost in the accident?

Jolene noticed everyone looking at her and scrunched up her face. "What?"

"Nothing," Morgan answered for them.

"I know what you're thinking and you're wrong. I can still use my paranormal gifts."

Jolene thrust her hand out as if to shoot off an energy spark. Nothing happened, and she put it in front of her frowning face. "Well, I think I can." She thrust it out again, harder this time.

"Hey, don't vaporize my favorite crystal lamp over there in the living room. You're pointing right at it," Johanna warned.

But she didn't need to worry about the lamp. Jolene couldn't muster any energy. No matter how hard she focused, the best she could do was produce a teeny, glowing pink drop which formed at the end of her fingertip then fell off, disappearing into nothing before it hit the floor.

The forlorn look on Jolene's face tugged at Morgan's heart. She put her arm around her little sister. "Don't worry. I'm sure it's just the effects of getting knocked out. I'm sure your gifts will come back."

She hoped her words were true. Jolene was the most powerful of all the sisters and they'd have a hard time defending themselves without her skills. Morgan made a mental note to try to develop her own defensive paranormal skill.

"So, what do we do now?" Luke asked. "There's at least two groups in town looking for the relic and if you guys don't have any clue at all, how can we possibly hope to find it before they do?"

"I wouldn't say we don't have any clue at all," Morgan said. "I think the rest of the epitaph might tell us something, even though we won't know what the bottom says."

Luke leaned back against the kitchen island and crossed his arms over his chest. "Okay, tell us what the rest of it was and let's see if we can figure it out."

Morgan repeated the epitaph.

When two become one, the healing's begun.
In my favorite place under the sun
Look to the west. I can finally rest.

Jake made a face. "What kind of a poem is that?"

"You should have seen some of the other ones on the other stones," Fiona said.

"It's not a very good poem. But if it's a clue, then I guess we should try to figure it out," Johanna added.

Luke looked skeptical. "How do we even know if it *is* a clue?"

"Ezra's ghost told me he left a clue before he died in the most important part of the graveyard," Celeste said.

"And, by all accounts, he thought he was pretty important," Fiona added.

"So, it stands to reason he left it on his gravestone," Morgan said.

"But how would he leave it on his gravestone?" Luke asked. "He'd already be dead when it was engraved."

"Yes, but he might have left instructions in his will," Celeste suggested.

Luke nodded. "True. We can check on that. And since we have nothing better to go on, we might as well try to figure out what it means."

"Well, it seems like the second line would be a pretty big clue," Jake said.

"*In my favorite place under the sun*," Johanna repeated. "Who knows where his favorite place was?"

"Maybe Thaddeus?" Morgan suggested.

Celeste made a face. "We could ask him, but his answers aren't always reliable."

"Maybe the first line is a hint at his favorite place," Celeste said.

"When two become one?" Morgan narrowed her eyes and looked up at the ceiling. "Where *does* two become one?"

"Maybe it has something to do with one of the roads out near the farm," Fiona suggested. "Like where two roads merge?"

Morgan shook her head. "No, I think it's something that has more meaning. His favorite place."

"And the bit about looking to the west," Jake said. "That's got to be a clue that the relic is hidden in the western section."

"Yeah, but of what?" Johanna chewed her bottom lip.

Celeste snapped her fingers. "I've got it! Thaddeus said that Ezra loved his wife, Lila-Mae. Remember, he said he was really upset when she died and threw himself into his pharmacy work."

"Yeah..." Morgan raised her brows at Celeste.

"Think about it. When do 'two become one'?" Celeste looked at them with wide eyes and when no one answered, she continued. "When they get married!"

Johanna smiled. "Of course! The second line makes perfect sense, then, because his favorite place would be where Ezra and Lila-Mae got married."

"You think that's where he hid the relic?" Jolene asked.

"It's a good place to start," Morgan said. "There's only one problem."

"What?"

"How do we figure out where Ezra and Lila-Mae got married?"

***

"I can help out with that." Jolene's face lit up with eagerness and she hurried out of the kitchen into the east parlor, motioning for them to follow.

Morgan slipped behind the desk next to Jolene while Fiona and Celeste stood in front of it. Johanna stationed her chair beside it and Luke and Jake hovered in the doorway. Morgan looked over her sister's shoulder as Jolene flipped open the laptop.

The login screen blinked at them.

Jolene frowned at it, her fingers poised over the keyboard. After a few seconds, she quickly typed a username and password.

Wrong username.

"I must have hit the wrong key." Jolene tried again.

Wrong username.

"Huh. What the heck is wrong with this thing?" Jolene's voice was edged with annoyance. She tried a few more combinations, punching the return key harder and harder with each failed attempt.

Finally, she looked up at them. "Okay, who changed my login?"

Morgan looked over at Fiona and Celeste, who both shrugged.

"No one changed it," Morgan said.

"Someone did ... or I maybe I can't remember it." Jolene's voice cracked. Johanna reached over and put a reassuring hand on Jolene's arm. "It's okay. That's just part of getting hit in the head. A good rest and you'll be fine."

Jolene looked uncertainly at her mother and Morgan's heart pinched for her. Would Jolene be fine?

"I'll get one of my carnelians to help." Fiona hurried out of the room. Her special gift with crystals and stones included a way with carnelian, an orange stone associated with healing. Fiona had used the stone several times in the past to speed up the recovery time for various wounds. Morgan hoped it would work just as well for a head injury.

Morgan leaned over and typed her login on the keyboard. "We can still get in. Now, where do we start?"

"Google." Jolene straightened in the chair and started typing, her disposition improving as her typing produced a list of articles on Ezra Finch.

Morgan squinted at the screen. She ran her index finger down the list. "I don't see anything here about the wedding."

"Well, I have work to do," Luke cut in. "I'll leave you girls to it, but don't go running off without telling me."

He shot Morgan a warning look, which she countered with an innocent smile. "Of course not. We would never do that." She leaned out from behind the desk and gave him a peck on the lips, then ducked her head back down toward the screen.

"I better get going, too," Jake said. "You girls are the experts at computer stuff." He headed toward the doorway, meeting up with Fiona, who had a bunched-up towel in her hand. She slipped into the hallway with him for a hasty good-bye kiss.

"Well, looks like it's just us girls." Fiona came back into the room and handed the towel to Jolene. "Put this on your head. The carnelians are inside."

Jolene accepted the towel. She opened it cautiously and peeked inside. Over her shoulder, Morgan could see the orange, glowing stones. Jolene wrapped it back up and applied it to her head like an ice pack.

"Look, here's an article on his pharmacy." Fiona, who had joined them behind the desk, pointed to an entry halfway down the screen.

Morgan clicked on it and scanned the article. "Gee, I guess he really was important."

"Yeah, and there's a picture of the pharmacy building. It was pretty small, but I don't remember seeing that anywhere in town," Fiona said.

"Let me see." Celeste leaned over the desk and they angled the laptop so she could see the screen. "Oh, that's right on the Finch farm. It's about two hundred feet from the house. I remember seeing a pile of debris I thought was an old chicken coop near the barn that fell down."

"It says here it burned." Morgan tapped the screen. "The police investigated, but didn't find anything suspicious. Old wiring, I guess. That was only about seven years ago."

"Interesting, but I don't see anything about him getting married," Jolene said.

"That information is probably too old to be in Google," Celeste pointed out. "He would have been married way before the internet even existed."

"Yeah, probably. But it's not too old to be in the town records, and those were just digitized and put in a database last year." Jolene put the towel down, turned the computer back toward her

116

and started typing furiously. "If I can just remember … there!"

Morgan bent over her shoulder to see an official-looking website. A search bar blinked at the top. Jolene typed in 'Finch' and a listing appeared on the screen.

"That's a lot to look through." Morgan pressed her lips together as she perused the list. It looked like every birth, death and marriage in the Finch family since the dawn of time was represented. She sensed an energy drain beside her and turned to look at Jolene, who appeared tired and pale. "You go lie down with that thing and I'll take it from here. You've done the important part."

Jolene stifled a yawn. "Maybe I'll just lie down on the couch in here. I don't want to miss out on anything."

Morgan slid into the chair as Jolene made her way to the couch. She squinted at the screen. "Okay, so let's see what we have here."

Fiona looked on over her shoulder. "This looks like the births, deaths and marriages. Maybe we can narrow it down to *just* marriages."

Morgan typed in 'Finch marriage' at the search bar and a new screen appeared. She scrolled back into the 1800s, where Ezra would have been married.

"Aha! Here it is, right here." Fiona tapped the screen with a red-polished fingernail." Ezra Finch married to Lila-Mae Finch ... place, St. Anne's Church."

"Isn't that the old medieval-looking church out on Fowler Road?" Celeste asked.

Fiona nodded. "Yep, that's the one. But it's been abandoned for years. Do you think that the relic would still be in there?"

Morgan shrugged and snapped the laptop cover closed. "There's only one way to find out."

Chapter Twelve

St Anne's church sat at the end of a rarely traveled road, surrounded by woods. The gothic-style stone structure still looked impressive, even though most of the windows were boarded up and a tree was growing out of one of them.

"This place has sure seen better days. How does a church become abandoned, anyway?" Fiona asked.

Celeste stared at the sagging roof. "It's too far out. Everyone started going to St. Michael's in town."

They circled the outside of the building, their feet crunching in the snow. The cathedral-style doors had big boards nailed in front of them so no one could get in. The back and side doors were also nailed shut.

"How do we get in?" Jolene asked.

Morgan tuned up her intuition. She turned slowly like a dowsing rod, looking for a way in. Instead of the familiar ping that would tell her which way to go, she felt a nagging buzz in her stomach. A buzz that told her they probably shouldn't have come to this creepy old church out in the woods at dusk.

"Hey, look!" Celeste interrupted Morgan's focus and she turned to see her pointing at a narrow window that had two boards missing. So much for using her intuition—maybe she should have just used her eyes.

Celeste was already over at the window, the bottom of which was waist height. She lifted her leg, straddled it, swung her other leg over, disappeared inside, then poked her head out. "Come on in!"

Jolene, who was shorter than Celeste, tried to hoist herself up and over, but failed on the first attempt.

"You should be at home resting," Morgan said, regretting her decision to let the obviously exhausted Jolene accompany them.

Jolene waved her hand. "I'm okay. Just a little tired. Besides, you guys might need me if we run into bad guys."

A funny feeling crept into Morgan's stomach as she watched Jolene hoist herself onto the window ledge and swing herself over. Would Jolene be able to help them if they ran into bad guys? Morgan let Fiona go next, then switched on her flashlight and followed her sisters through the window.

The pungent, musky smell of dry wood and mildew hit Morgan's nose as she watched the dust motes they'd stirred up dance in the light of the flashlight. She stifled a cough and surveyed the nearly empty church.

"It sure does look weird with all the pews gone," Fiona said.

"That's for sure." Celeste aimed her flashlight in a slow circle, illuminating the rest of the church. There wasn't much to illuminate. Most everything had been taken, even the lights. Morgan aimed her light at the front. The altar was still there and behind it, the wall showed a lighter spot where the cross had hung for decades. Creepy. A layer of dust had settled on the floor—no one had been there in years.

"Look, they even took out the stained glass windows." Jolene stood at one of the window openings, now just covered with plywood. Morgan remembered the colorful windows that had illuminated the church with jewel-like light. They were gone now, probably taken when they closed the church.

"If they took everything, then what are the chances the relic is still here?" Fiona asked.

"Depends on where he hid it." Jolene started toward the altar. "Sometimes they had a hiding spot up under the altar."

"Really? Where'd you hear that? I never knew about it," Fiona said.

Jolene turned back with a half-shrug. "I heard it somewhere." She tapped the side of her head. "Maybe my photographic memory is returning."

They followed her to the front, the cathedral ceiling and empty room amplifying the echoes of their footsteps on the marble floor.

"*Meow!*"

Morgan turned toward the sound, her eyes widening as she recognized their white cat. "Belladonna! How did *you* get here?"

Morgan searched her sisters' faces, but they looked as puzzled as she was. They were miles from home. It wasn't possible for the cat to just walk here. But it wasn't unusual, either. Belladonna had shown up at sites far from home before.

"Maybe she hides in the car," Fiona offered.

Jolene bent down to pet the cat and soft purrs echoed off the walls. "Well, we can't do anything now. She's already here. We'll just make sure to load her in the car when we leave."

They crawled around on the altar, tapping and pressing on the wood, looking for something hollow that might indicate a compartment under the floor.

"Hey, maybe it's under here." Celeste moved a pile of debris and a mouse skittered out from underneath. "Ack!"

"*Merrrp!*" Belladonna took off after it like a shot. The mouse let out a tiny squeak as it raced to the wall and flattened itself to fit under the molding. Belladonna hit the wall a split-second later, then jumped back and glared at the place the mouse had disappeared into.

"Tough luck, Belladonna," Fiona said to the cat, who continued to stare intently at the piece of wall.

"I'm glad she didn't catch it." Celeste gingerly poked at the debris, then moved it aside to see if the floor held a secret compartment. "I don't need her leaving another mouse head in front of me."

"Mew." Scratch. Scratch.

"Give it a rest, Belladonna. That mouse is not going to be stupid enough to come back out," Jolene called over her shoulder as the girls resumed their search.

But Belladonna didn't give it a rest. She continued to meow and scratch in the most annoying manner as the girls continued to search for a secret compartment.

"I don't think there's any secret compartment with a hidden relic here. We must have gotten the clue wrong again." Morgan's heart sank. She looked around the altar. Had they covered every inch? She stood and brushed the dirt off the knees of her jeans. "Let's go home. I'll get Belladonna."

Morgan walked over to the wall and attempted to pick Belladonna up.

"Breee!" Belladonna jumped away and swatted at Morgan angrily.

"Hey, cut that out." Morgan made another grab for her.

"*Merow!*" Belladonna scratched frantically at the wall.

Morgan squatted next to her. "What's this?"

The tile next to the wall had several cracks. Morgan picked at the edge with her nail, lifting a section up. It looked like there was something underneath. Slowly, she pried up the rest of the tile, her heartbeat picking up speed as she saw a copper ring underneath it.

Fiona, Celeste and Jolene had come over and were standing behind her.

"Check this out." Morgan pointed to the ring.

"What's that?" Fiona asked.

"It looks like there's something under there." Celeste curled her finger under the ring and pulled, but it didn't budge. "Maybe this is where the relic is hidden."

"I think we need to pull up more tiles."

The girls got busy pulling up the next tile. Belladonna sat a foot away, licking her paw and running it behind her ear.

"I just hope that mouse doesn't come out," Celeste said as they pried up another marble tile.

They pried up another tile and now Morgan could see that the ring was attached to some sort of trap door or cover, about eight inches square. She held her breath, grabbed the ring and pulled.

It creaked open, revealing a shallow, dark compartment. Morgan practically laid on the floor to peer in, but it was too dark. Without saying a word, she extended her hand and Celeste slapped a flashlight into it. Morgan aimed the light into the compartment.

"Hey, there's—"

Something skidded across the floor, spinning to a stop in front of Morgan. Her heart froze when she recognized it as a licorice. A Black Crow licorice. She heard a hollow click and the words:

"Hand over the relic or die."

Chapter Thirteen

Morgan couldn't see the intruder's face, only his dark silhouette against the thin, sliver of light from the open window in the back of the church.

She glanced down at the licorice. She didn't need to see his face to know what he was—a cold-blooded killer.

Beside her, Jolene fisted her hands on her hips. "Who the heck are you?"

"You don't know who I am?" the intruder said in a subdued baritone. "That's funny, because I know who you girls are. You're the ones who killed my brother and I won't have his death be in vain. Hand over the relic. Now."

Morgan's brow furrowed. "Killed your brother? What are you talking about?"

"Don't play coy with me." The intruder took a menacing step forward.

Morgan's stomach clenched. She glanced down into the hidden compartment, then slammed the lid and stepped in front of it. Thoughts whirled through her brain. Clearly this man was the licorice killer and he'd been following them to find the relic. But was he aligned with Bly or just in it for himself?

And who was his brother?

She didn't have time to contemplate that, though. They needed to get out of the situation.

Her eyes slid over to Jolene, who was flexing her hand as if to summon her paranormal powers. Morgan wondered if she would be successful or if they would have to fight the man off without Jolene's skills. She shifted her gaze back to the intruder, and wondered what kind of paranormal powers he would unleash on them and how they could combat him.

"Now!" The intruder jerked the gun toward the box and for the first time, Morgan noticed that he held his left hand slightly behind his back. Was he holding some sort of paranormal contraption? She hoped it wasn't one of those energy-draining geodes the bearded guys behind the museum had used on her.

Morgan let her attention slide to her sisters. Fiona had scooped up some small pebbles in her hand and Celeste was inching her way to the right. The tension in her body told Morgan she was ready to launch into one of her karate kicks at any time.

"Why do you want the relic so bad, anyway?" Morgan figured it was best to keep him talking while her sisters fanned out around him.

"I have my reasons," The intruder ground out. "Now, move aside."

He took another step toward Morgan.

Jolene flexed her hand faster.

Morgan glanced down at the compartment. "Well, I don't know what all the fuss is. What are you going to do with a little thing like this?"

She could see the intruders face now and he wasn't nearly as menacing as she would have expected. He didn't have a beard, for one, and his tanned face had a look of sincerity. In fact, he seemed almost sad, like he didn't want to be holding a gun on her. She hoped her intuition wasn't failing her because from what it was telling her, the man was no threat at all.

"I don't know what you're playing at." He took another step and she noticed he was chewing something—a Black Crow licorice, no doubt. "You know right well what to do with that. You killed for it."

Morgan's brows mashed together. *Who did he think they'd killed?* "Why do you keep saying that? We didn't kill anyone."

The intruder laughed. "I know all about you girls. You're cold-blooded, paranormal killers. You'll do anything to enhance your powers, including killing an innocent man."

"What are you talking about? You're the one who is a killer," Morgan said.

His eyes narrowed. "What are *you* talking about? I didn't kill anyone."

"Sure, you did. Right in downtown, on Beach street. He had a paranormal energy burn, and I know it was you because I saw the licorice beside his body." Morgan gestured toward the man's licorice-chewing mouth.

Confusion washed across his face. "You're trying to trick me. *You're* the paranormal killers."

"We are not killers!" Jolene punctuated the last word by thrusting her fingers out toward the man. Normally, a stream of potent energy would fly from them, but now, only a small dribble of dots slowly floated out toward him.

He reacted by bringing his left hand out from behind his back, revealing some sort of reflective mirror gizmo. The dots of energy bounced off the mirror and shot straight back at Jolene.

"Ouch!" Jolene grabbed her arm where she'd been hit with the ricochet of her own energy.

Fiona had reacted quickly. Before the energy could bounce back at Jolene, she flung the stones in her hand toward the man. But he was quicker. He pivoted, holding the mirror in her direction, and the stones bounced off it and sped back toward Fiona. They hit her jacket, making little singe marks. Down feathers poked out of two of them and fluttered into the air.

Morgan felt relieved that Fiona's attempts to use the stones as weapons hadn't been too successful. Otherwise, she might have been badly hurt. But now it was up to Morgan and Celeste, and neither of them had any paranormal fighting abilities. Morgan did have one thing, though—her intuition. And she used it now to sense which direction the man would strike. He came toward her and she jumped to the left while at the same time, Celeste kicked out toward his gun hand, connecting with it and sending the gun flying.

"Hey!" He turned toward Celeste, his fists up as if to hit her. Then he hesitated. Morgan could see emotions warring on his face as he stared at Celeste. The hesitation gave her the advantage and she lowered her shoulder, then plowed into him like a linebacker and knocked him to the floor.

Fiona ran for the gun.

Morgan leapt on the man's chest, Celeste on his legs.

Jolene grabbed a length of rope from the pile of debris Celeste had moved earlier. They turned him over on his stomach and then secured his hands behind his back. Morgan was surprised, and suspicious, that he didn't offer much resistance. They flipped him back over. Surprisingly, he didn't struggle.

"Okay. You girls win."

Something in the man's voice niggled at Morgan. He sounded resigned. Too resigned. And then she realized something odd. The man hadn't used any paranormal moves on them aside from the mirror. Morgan suspected he didn't have any paranormal skills. So, just who was he?

"I suppose you'll kill me too, now," he said as they moved him to a sitting position. He screwed his eyes shut and hung his head. "Go ahead and get it over with."

The girls exchanged confused looks. He was acting very odd for a killer. Did he really think *they* had killed someone?

"I told you. We're not killers," Morgan said.

"Well, not unless we have to in order to defend ourselves," Jolene added.

The man looked up at Morgan and she noticed his clear, green eyes were shiny with tears. What kind of a killer started crying upon being captured by girls? Was this some kind of trick? But Morgan's gut instinct told her the man was sincere.

"I'm sure you didn't have to defend yourselves from my brother. He wasn't a violent man. I saw the burn mark on him and I know that's the sort of mark paranormal killers make," the man said.

Morgan's brows shot up. "Your brother? You mean to tell me Hale Swain was your brother?"

The man hung his head and nodded.

"Then you must be Gunner Swain ... the archaeologist," Celeste said.

Another sad nod.

132

"But your brother had a map to the Finch Farm. Why would an archeologist and his brother be interested in that if it wasn't to find the relic?" Jolene asked.

"And why follow us around?" Fiona added.

"You just don't get it!" Swain's voice was pitched with anger. "All you care about is using the relic for your own evil purposes. Didn't you ever think it might be used for good? To help people?"

The sisters stared at him, surprised by his outburst.

"No, I didn't think so," he continued. "Well, what does it matter now? You'll kill me just like you killed Hale, and Mom will die all alone. I've failed her." Swain's voice cracked and he hung his head. Morgan's heart softened as she watched a fat tear drop onto his lap.

"Oh, for crying out loud, cut the whining." Jolene rolled her eyes. "We aren't going to kill you."

"You aren't? But you killed Hale." Swain looked at them skeptically.

"For the umpteenth time, we didn't kill your brother." Morgan felt sorry for him and her intuition was telling her he wasn't the enemy. She didn't know how far she could trust her intuition, but she doubted he'd killed his own brother. "But

I saw his body ... and a black licorice beside it, just like those in your pocket."

Swain looked down at the Black Crow licorice box peeking out of his top pocket. "Yeah, I was there. Hale had taken off ... he was always so impetuous. Anyway, he rushed off with the map and I went out to find him. I found him, all right, but not before someone else got him first. I must have dropped the licorice. I wasn't really paying much attention after I saw what had been done to him."

"Someone killed him, either to keep him from getting to the relic or to find out what he knew about it," Celeste suggested. "But why did you think it was us?"

Swain shrugged. "I'd heard about you girls through some of my underground contacts and when I saw the burn on him, I knew no normal person could have done that, so I just assumed it was you. I knew you lived here and I figured you'd be after the relic. So I followed you around figuring you'd know where it is."

"We are," Jolene said. "But we wouldn't kill for it. That doesn't explain why you and your brother are so hot for it, though. Were you that eager to make a big discovery and get in the papers?"

Swain scrunched up his face. "Is that what you think this is about? Trust me, the relic itself isn't any big discovery as far as the archeological community is concerned. In fact, it probably doesn't mean squat to anyone outside of the paranormal community. But we don't really care about any of that. Hale was so eager to help our mother get better that he rushed off ... well, I suppose now it doesn't matter. What's to become of me?"

Morgan's heart melted. She believed Swain was sincere—he wasn't after the relic for personal gain. He wanted it because somehow it could help his mother. She didn't know what was wrong with his mother, but she could sympathize.

She glanced at her sisters. "Well, since we aren't killers or kidnappers and you don't seem to be a threat, I guess we'll just let you go."

Fiona, Celeste and Jolene nodded and Morgan bent down to untie his hands.

He looked up at them incredulously. "Really?"

"Yes. I don't know what you heard about us, but we're the good guys. We're just after the relic to keep it out of the hands of people who would use it for bad intent."

"But if you didn't kill Hale, then who did?"

"There are other paranormals who aren't as nice as we are. They want the relic, too. One of them killed your brother." Jolene frowned at Swain, who was rubbing his wrists. "You're not a paranormal, are you?"

He shook his head. "No. I'm just a simple archaeologist. I found out about the relic through my contacts."

"And this." Morgan gingerly picked up the mirror weapon. It looked ancient. The frame was bronze with symbols around it, and the middle piece which she'd thought was a mirror appeared to be mica. "Did you get this from your contacts?"

Swain nodded. "I paid a pretty penny for it. It's Mayan. It's said to bounce energy back at the sender. And it worked a treat too, didn't it? I wasn't sure if it really would."

"Yes, it did." Morgan looked at her sisters. "This could come in handy."

"I might be willing to trade it for the relic." Swain started toward the hidden compartment.

Morgan stepped in front of him. "Not so fast. We didn't say we'd let you have the relic."

"Oh, I don't want to keep it. I just need it for my Mom and then I'll give it right back to you guys."

Jolene snorted. "Right. Like we'd trust you with it."

Swain looked hurt ... and desperate. "You can come with me. Please. She's dying."

Morgan's heart pinched. Clearly, Swain new more about the relic than they did. He thought it had some healing powers. Morgan wished she could help him.

Celeste must have felt sorry for him, too. She looked at Morgan, then at Swain, her face pinched. "Maybe we could try to help him out? I mean, it can't hurt. And anyway, I'm dying to see what this relic is ... sounds like it has something to do with healing."

Morgan pressed her lips together as Celeste started toward the hidden compartment. "Don't bother."

Celeste's brow creases as she turned and looked at Morgan. "What? Why not?"

"The relic isn't here. The compartment was empty."

Chapter Fourteen

Jolene's brow creased. "What do you mean? It was empty the whole time?"

"Yep. I was just about to tell you that when Indiana Jones here burst in on us." Morgan tilted her head toward Swain.

Swain marched over to the compartment and opened it. He bent over and peered inside, then slammed the lid shut.

"I don't believe it." He paced the length of the altar, running his hands through his short, dark-blond hair. "It seemed like we were so close."

Morgan raised her left brow at him. "We?"

He shrugged sheepishly. "Well, *you*. I was mostly following, but don't take that to mean that I don't know how to find something. I am an archaeologist, after all. But I figured why do the work when I could let you do it for me?"

Celeste narrowed her eyes at him. "You had a map. So why were you following *us*?"

Swain looked at them as he paced. "It seemed like you girls had some sort of an advantage. Plus it's your home turf. The map led me to the graveyard at the Finch farm and when I saw you there, I figured I'd let you do all the work and just follow behind."

"So, you did look in the cornerstone before us, then." Fiona said.

"Yep. It was empty."

"This is frustrating," Jolene said. "These clues keep leading us to the wrong place."

"Maybe this is the right place and someone got here before us," Swain said.

Morgan shook her head. "No. When we came in there was a layer of undisturbed dust on the floor. No one has been here in decades."

"We must have interpreted the clues wrong," Celeste said.

"What, exactly, were the clues?" Swain asked.

"The epitaph on the gravestone," Jolene answered. "Of course there was that last line ..."

"Last line?" Swain pivoted to look at Jolene. "Sounds like you have some sort of question about it."

"We're not sure exactly what it is," Jolene admitted.

"Let's just go read it, then." Swain started toward the exit.

"That's the thing." Morgan's voice stopped him in his tracks and he turned back around to face them again. "We can't."

"Why not?" he asked.

His eyebrows crept higher and higher on his forehead as they told him about the freak snowstorm in the graveyard, how the gravestone was smashed to pieces and how they couldn't read the last line since it was buried.

Swain was thoughtful for a few seconds, then said, "So these bad guys ... they must think the clue is on the gravestone, too, then. I mean, if they were the ones that created the storm and smashed the stone."

"Yes, that's what we think," Fiona said.

"But is it really?" Swain asked. "I mean, *why* do you all think that?"

"Well, you said yourself the map leads there and Celeste ... well ..." Morgan hesitated. Should she tell Swain Celeste talked to ghosts? Seeing as he'd already admitted he knew they had paranormal gifts, she didn't see the sense in keeping it a secret. "She talked to Ezra's ghost."

"Ezra Finch? He was in my research, too. I think he is the key." Swain started pacing again. "But maybe we are going about this all wrong. Maybe he hid it in plain sight."

"Here you go with the '*we*' again," Jolene said. "There is no *we*. You just tried to shoot us!"

"That was an honest mistake. I thought you'd killed Hale. But now I can see that you aren't killers." Swain held up his chafed wrists. "Because you let me go. So we should team up."

Jolene scrunched up her face. "I don't know about that. We usually work solo."

"Yeah, you've been doing a great job so far." Swain waved his hand at the empty compartment.

Morgan looked down at it and grimaced. He did have a point.

But maybe you are stuck on one track," Swain continued. "You might need a different perspective. This happens in archaeology sometimes—you get stuck going down the wrong path, and sometimes you just need to reevaluate what you *think* you know."

"What do you mean?" Celeste asked.

"Well, so far, you've been operating under the assumption that Ezra Finch hid the relic somewhere. In the cornerstone or this box, but maybe he hid it in plain sight."

"Plain sight?"

"Yeah, out in the open, where it's not obvious that it's something special. You girls know the family history better than me. Is there somewhere he might have put it where it would seem like it was just normally supposed to be there?"

Morgan glanced at her sisters. "Umm ... we're not sure."

"What about that guy you keep visiting in the nursing home. His grandson, is it? Maybe he would know," Swain suggested.

"It's his great-grandson," Jolene said. "And he's not really that reliable with his information. Plus he doesn't know Ezra had a magical relic."

"He doesn't necessarily need to know it's a *magic* relic. You can ask if his great-grandfather had one…" Swain narrowed his eyes at them. "You know, where one would normally be."

Morgan shifted her weight on her feet and looked at the ground.

Swain stopped pacing and gave them a sideways look. "I'm sure you can name several places the relic would be camouflaged or where it wouldn't call attention to it being something special, right?"

"Of course we can." Morgan avoided eye contact. How could they know where the relic would look 'normal' if they didn't even know what it was?

"*Meow*."

Morgan had almost forgotten about the cat, but here she was, weaving her way around Swain's ankles. He bent down to pet her and a low purr reverberated around the room.

"So, it seems like we can help each other figure this out," Swain said. "I say we team up."

Jolene shook her head. "I don't think that's in our best interest. Besides, it sounds like that would benefit you more than it would us. You don't have much to offer us."

"Au contraire. I think you need my help. Don't forget that I'm an archaeologist and am used to deciphering clues. I've brought more artifacts to the light of day than any other archaeologist this decade."

Celeste jerked her head up to look at Swain. "Light Of Day—so that boat in the cove is yours!"

Swain nodded. "Yes."

Morgan could feel Celeste tensing, her knees slightly bent as if she was readying to get into her karate stance.

"And that poor woman on the boat," Celeste said. "What did you do to her?"

"*Do* to her? That's my mother." A cloud of sadness passed over Swain's face. "She's sick. That's why I want the relic—to heal her. I'm not interested in getting credit for it or even keeping it. In fact, you girls can have it after I'm done."

"What's wrong with her?" Morgan asked softly.

"Cancer. Stage III." Swain turned his desperate eyes on Morgan. "Don't you see? The relic is my only hope to save her."

Morgan's heart melted. She sensed he was telling the truth, and the truth was they were running out of leads. She could relate to his desire to cure his mother—it wasn't that long ago that she thought her own mother was lost to her forever. If they had a chance to help cure Swain's mother and they didn't take it, Morgan would never forgive herself. Most importantly, though, her gut instincts were telling her that joining forces with the archaeologist was the right thing to do.

"I think we should team up with him." Morgan eyed her sisters hopefully. "He'll probably just follow us around anyway if we don't. This way, we can keep an eye on him."

Jolene sighed. "I guess you're right.

"And Belladonna seems to approve of him." Fiona pointed to the cat, who was still enjoying Swains attention. Belladonna took a moment out from her slit-eyed purring to wink at Morgan.

"And he does have that mica thing that could really come in handy against paranormal bad guys," Celeste pointed out.

Swain broke out into a smile. "You girls are making the right decision. Plus teaming up with me will probably benefit you girls as much, if not more, than it will benefit me."

"How's that?" Jolene asked.

"Because I know what the relic actually is."

***

"A mortar and pestle?" Morgan frowned at Swain. "But those aren't very rare. I have several of them right in my shop."

"Yeah, how would we know if we even had the right one?" Jolene asked as she passed Swain a mug of coffee across the island of their kitchen, where they'd all come to after they left the church.

145

Swain accepted the tea and, taking the rectangular box of licorice out of his pocket, he tipped it towards the girls. "Licorice?"

"No, thanks." The four of them declined.

Swain put the box back in his pocket and leaned over to grab his coffee. A Black Crow licorice fell out and bounced on the counter.

"Darn things are always falling out." Swain picked up the licorice and dropped it into his cup of coffee.

"That explains why we were always finding them everywhere," Morgan said. "You left a trail like Hansel and Gretel."

Swain grimaced. "Anyway, the mortar and pestle we're after is special. It's imbued with potent healing properties."

Celeste snapped her fingers. "That makes perfect sense. Ezra was a pharmacist and back in the day he would have used a mortar and pestle to compound his remedies. Even the chemical ones."

"No wonder he was so popular," Fiona said. "His remedies were magic."

Morgan's left brow ticked up. "Boy, I wouldn't mind having one of those in my shop."

Swain winked. "Maybe one of your mortar and pestles *is* the one?"

Morgan's eyes widened. "Could it be?"

Swain shook his head. "No. I don't think so. I think you'd notice right away that the remedies

146

you made were very powerful. Besides this one, I'm told, is easily recognizable as being different."

"Different how?" Luke, who had been sitting in the corner silently, narrowed his eyes at Swain. He hadn't been too happy that the girls had taken Swain in, but like the rest of them, he'd learned to trust Morgan's instincts—which he was now doing reluctantly.

Swain tipped the licorice box in Luke's direction. Luke shook his head and Swain shrugged, then picked a licorice out of the box and popped it in his mouth.

"*That*, I'm not entirely sure about," he said as he chewed. "I figure it's marked in some way so that one would know it's not just an everyday mortar and pestle."

Jolene shifted the carnelian-filled towel she was holding to her head into her left hand and picked up her cell phone with her right. "I can text Brody to see if I can get a list of the items stolen from the museum. Maybe there will be something obvious, but I think we need something more specific to go on that just that it's 'different'."

"Maybe there's a clue to that in the epitaph on Ezra's gravestone, too," Celeste suggested.

"The bottom line?" Johanna asked.

"Maybe," Celeste answered. "Too bad we don't know what it said."

"We could ask Thaddeus," Fiona suggested. "He might remember, or maybe he has some paperwork from when the stone was engraved?"

"I just wish I could remember. I *should* be able to." Jolene sounded defeated.

"You're probably exhausted," Morgan said. "In fact, I'm pretty tired myself. We should all get to bed early tonight. I want to get started first thing tomorrow."

"Good idea. With all the excitement in the graveyard and at the church, we forgot to stop by *Sticks and Stones*." Fiona glanced out the window at the dark night. "It's too late now, but we need to go first thing tomorrow. We should be wearing those in case things get cagey with Bly."

Johanna nodded. "You girls better make that a priority. Those amulets could save your lives."

"That's right," Luke said. "You girls need the protection."

Jolene let out a loud sigh. "Especially since my unique gifts don't seem to be working. I can't even defend us against a child."

"Well, at least we have this gizmo now." Fiona pointed to the mica mirror.

"I was wondering what that thing was," Luke said. "What does it do?"

Morgan explained how the ancient object's surface was mica and it would reflect energy back

148

at the sender. "So basically, whatever you try to do to your opponent ends up happening to you."

Luke's lips flattened into a thin line. "Wait a minute, are you saying Swain was able to redirect what little paranormal powers you have back at you *and* he had a gun? How did you guys manage to defeat him?"

Swain swallowed his licorice hard. "That is rather embarrassing."

"It was luck on our part," Morgan said. "Celeste took a big chance and chopped him with a karate kick."

"Surely a big guy like Swain could have taken her out?" Luke glanced at Swain's broad shoulders and muscular arms.

"Probably," Celeste said. "But he hesitated and that gave me the opening I needed to tackle him. Then Morgan and I jumped on him and we tied him up."

Morgan's eyes narrowed. "Hey, why *did* you hesitate, anyway?"

Swain flushed and dipped his head. "My mother told me never to hit a woman, so when it came down to it, I couldn't fight back."

Luke burst out laughing. Well, I guess chivalry was your downfall." He gave Swain a friendly punch and Morgan's heart lifted at the show of camaraderie. Luke had been understandably aloof when they'd brought Swain home and she was glad to see his frozen demeanor was thawing.

Luke's job was to be suspicious of strangers and to protect the girls from them, but Morgan knew in her gut that Swain was not a threat. Not only that, but Belladonna curled up and purring in Swains lap was the only reference he needed. The cat was an extraordinary judge of character.

"About your Mom ..." Johanna turned her concerned, amber eyes on Swain. "I think we should bring her here. It can't be good for her to be on that boat. We have plenty of room."

"Oh, I don't know." Swain looked around at them.

"It might be smart," Luke said. "Bly is going to find out that you guys are partnered up now and he might retaliate. In fact, I'm a bit surprised he hasn't done something already. Your boat is out in the cove unprotected, like a sitting duck."

A look of alarm passed over Swain's face. "I hadn't thought about that." He turned to Johanna. "But I don't want to intrude."

"Nonsense." Johanna waved her hand dismissively. "It will give me something to do."

"Okay." Swain glanced around tentatively. "But she is very sick and has a private nurse."

"We know all about sick," Johanna assured him. "And there's plenty of room for the nurse, too. Plus, you won't have to worry about her being safe if she's here. We have lots of protection. You can focus on finding the relic."

"Well, that settles it then." Swain brushed his hands together. "Sounds like this is going to be a great partnership."

"Don't get too excited," Luke said. "Now that Bly and Overton know you guys are working together, they're sure to want to knock you all out of commission. We need to find that relic fast before someone else ends up dead."

Chapter Fifteen

Fiona stood in the doorway of *Sticks and Stones* and basked in the familiar sights, smells and sounds. The cottage, which had been in her family for centuries, had been one of her favorite places since childhood. When she'd grown up, she and Morgan had turned it into a shop with Morgan's herbal remedies on one side and Fiona's healing crystal jewelry on the other.

The cottage was off the beaten path. It was the off-season now with no tourists about, so the cottage was blanketed in silence. A single bird tweeted in the barren trees outside as Fiona breathed in the earthy smell of herbs and old wood.

The morning light filtered in through the window, illuminating the hand-hewn pine counter that doubled as Morgan's work area and the place where they rang up purchases.

Fiona started toward her workbench on the far end of the room, eliciting a creak from the dry wood floor as she crossed.

Morgan rushed in behind her, slamming the door shut against a gust of cold air and snow. "Gosh, it's cold out."

"And in here." Fiona's words came out in a cloud of condensation. "We should turn the thermostat up."

Morgan did as she was told. Noquitt was a summer tourist destination. That's when the girls did most of their shop business. In the winter, they came to the shop infrequently to fill the few orders they got from their regulars. They kept the heat on low when they weren't there, a habit ingrained in their thrifty, Maine Yankee blood.

The heat whooshed on. Fiona pulled off her gloves and rubbed her hands together as she surveyed her workbench. She'd been there just last week, working on the amulets and another project for herself—a sterling silver dragonfly necklace with iridescent golden-yellow citrine wings.

She didn't know what had prompted her to make the necklace—the idea had just come to her. Once it was stuck in her head, she had to get the piece designed. She pushed the piece aside and sat down at that table. There was no time for that now. She had to focus on the amulets.

"I feel like we should be out looking for the relic, but I do have some customer orders and the amulets are important." Morgan, who was now standing in front of her tall apothecary chest looking at the glass jars of herbs, echoed Fiona's thoughts.

"I know. I'll try to hurry ... I just have a few adjustments to make." Fiona plugged in her soldering iron and rummaged in the desk for the tools she would need.

"I hope the others get Swain's mother settled at home okay." Morgan pulled a glass jar filled with brown twigs off the shelf.

"I left some carnelians with instructions at home so they can start applying them right away," Fiona said. "It will be strange to have guests, but I think Mom was glad to have someone to 'mother' in the house. Since she's been home, we've been the ones mothering her and I don't think she likes it very much."

Johanna's seven-year imprisonment under Dr. Bly's hand had left her almost lifeless. Since she'd been home, she had made enormous improvements, but it was true that girls had been a bit overprotective and Fiona had noticed her mother getting more and more aggravated with them as her health improved.

"Another reason I wanted to come here this morning is that I felt like Jolene could use a morning to sleep in," Morgan said.

"That accident took a lot out of her and she hasn't rested. It must be emotionally draining for her to not have her paranormal gifts working." Fiona pressed her lips together. "Of course, it would be a lot less stressful on her if my shotgun rocks actually worked."

"You just need to believe and they will," Morgan said.

Fiona glanced at the dragonfly necklace. That's just what her father had always told her when she was a little girl. She just had to believe. The memory of her father, who had died years ago, brought a smile to her lips. He had been good with rocks, too. That's what had gotten Fiona interested in them. She could remember many afternoons spent with him going over the different types of crystals and their special properties.

And the dragonflies ... her gaze stole over to the necklace again. There always seemed to be dragonflies around when she'd been with her father. It was almost as if he'd had a way of attracting them. A few times, he'd joked that a dragonfly should have been his family crest.

Maybe that was what had prompted her to make the necklace. Old memories surfacing.

Her thoughts were interrupted by the door opening, which surprised her. She didn't think any shoppers would have been coming out this way.

A young woman with wavy, strawberry blonde hair that hung to her waist came through the door. A gust of wind swirled in with her, curling around her ankles and depositing a pile of snow on the floor as she turned to shut the door behind her.

"*Meow!*" Belladonna slipped through the crack of the door just before the woman closed it. The cat looked up at the woman, her ice-blue eyes narrowing to luminescent slits. "*Hiss!*"

Belladonna hopped sideways, away from the surprised woman, then ran under a chair on the far side of the room where she crouched and stared out at the room.

"Sorry." Fiona exchanged a look with Morgan and she knew her sister was wondering the same thing. How the heck did the cat get here?

"I don't know what is wrong with that cat." Morgan apologized. "Can we help you?"

"I hope so." The woman looked warily over at Belladonna as she walked forward, giving the cat a wide berth.

Something niggled Fiona's memory—the woman looked familiar. "Do we know each other?"

The woman smiled. "Yes, I'm Wendy North. Thaddeus Finch's health aide. We met at the nursing home."

"Oh, that's right," Fiona said. "I didn't recognize you with your hair down like that. You look different. What can we do for you?"

"Thaddeus told me about your shop and I thought I'd come in and see what you had. I'm looking for a necklace."

"Oh. Well, I use a variety of crystals. I can make pretty much anything you want." Fiona waved her hand over at the jewelry case where various items were on display.

Wendy narrowed storm-cloud gray eyes at the case. Her lips pressed together as she scanned the rows of jewelry. She shook her head. "No, I don't see anything that appeals to me here."

"Oh, is there something in particular you are looking for?" Fiona asked.

Wendy's hair swirled about her upper body as she swung around to look at Fiona's workspace. She pointed at the amulets that Fiona was working on. "Something like that would be perfect."

"That's obsidian," Fiona said.

"They're lovely. Are they for sale?" Wendy asked.

"These particular ones are spoken for, but I might have something in stock. If not, I can certainly make you one." Fiona walked over the old, oak map chest where she kept her stock and rummaged in the chest, opening drawer after drawer to look for an obsidian necklace.

"So, how is Thaddeus today?" Morgan asked from the other side of the shop.

"Oh, he's okay. He has his good and bad days." Wendy waved her hand and a pile of papers on the table near the chair Belladonna was crouching under fluttered off and floated to the floor. Belladonna let out a low guttural growl and a hiss. "I'm afraid you can't put much stock in what he says, though, so the answers he gave you the other day might not be true."

"Oh, we know about that. We're just old friends of the family trying to engage him to get him to talk about things he's interested in," Morgan said. Fiona knew this wasn't quite true, but she figured her sister didn't want Wendy knowing the real reason they were visiting Finch.

Fiona opened the last drawer. A beautiful obsidian necklace with a large stone lay right on top. "How about this one?" She turned toward Wendy, the black stone sparking off the light as it twirled from a silver chain.

"Very nice. I'll take it." Wendy reached out and snatched the necklace from Fiona, then swirled her way over to the cash register. She paid Morgan, who put the necklace in a gift bag.

At the door, Wendy turned back to face them. "Your shop is lovely. Thanks for taking the time to dig out the necklace for me."

"Thank you," Fiona said. "Say 'hi' to Thaddeus for us."

"I will." Wendy reached for the doorknob and Belladonna hissed, causing the woman's brows to mash together. "I guess your cat doesn't like me."

"She's persnickety," Morgan apologized.

Wendy narrowed her eyes in the direction of the chair and cracked the door open. The wind blew the door wide, gusting into the shop and setting papers and herbs flying in the air.

"Meow!" Belladonna flew out from under the chair and raced around the shop. Chasing the papers and herbs, she leapt into the air, twisting and turning, then plopped onto the ground and raced around the edge of the shop again.

"Hey, cut that out," Morgan said as the door slammed shut. She tried to intercept the cat, but failed. Belladonna made one more loop around the shop, hopping up into the jewelry drawer Fiona had left open and swatting out an earring that she proceeded to bat around the floor.

"Give that back." Fiona chased the cat to the back of the room, through the bathroom and then back out front where Belladonna finally batted the earring so hard it sailed into a crack between the old floorboards and wall.

Fiona crouched at the wall, stuck the nail of her finger in and tried to pry the earring out.

"Nice going, Belladonna." Fiona glared at the cat, who was all wide eyes and innocence perched on a chair, grooming her right paw. "It's stuck and I can't get it out."

"I don't know what's gotten into her lately." Morgan stood looking at the cat, her hands fisted on her hips. "But we really don't have time for this. We need to get back home and pick up Jolene and Celeste and get to the nursing home."

"I know." Fiona stood, brushing the dust off her knees. "I'll just finish up the last repair. The necklaces need to sit for a while to let the metal harden up, but we can swing back and get them after we visit Finch."

"Sounds like a plan, but please hurry." Morgan glanced at her watch. "We don't want to give Bly too much time to work on his plan to find the relic ... or to stop us from finding it."

Chapter Sixteen

Celeste had spent a restless night, filled with dreams of wrestling energy-infused mortars and pestles away from paranormals with bad intent. When she finally woke up, the sun had already risen and a quick glance into the driveway showed her that Morgan and Fiona were gone.

Luke and Swain, however, were not. She could hear the low sounds of their voices downstairs. She couldn't make out what they were saying, but assumed they must have been making plans to transfer Swain's mother. She could hear her mother bossing Jolene around as they prepared the rooms down at the end of the hall. A smile flitted across her lips as she pictured how exasperated Jolene must be getting—her little sister didn't like being told what to do.

Celeste was glad they were helping Swain. He seemed like a good guy. His motive to help his mother was selfless and if Morgan's instincts said they should work with him, then that was good enough for her.

Hopefully, they could find the relic, help Swain's Mom and then hand it over to Dorian, who would keep it safe in some secret government hiding place.

If only they could figure out where the relic was.

Celeste sat on her bed with a sigh. She felt like she could help out more. She knew Ezra left a clue because he'd told her himself, but things would be a lot easier if he would just come out and *tell* her where it was. Her fists clenched in frustration. What good was her special gift if she couldn't contact these ghosts whenever she wanted?

"Why so glum?"

The voice startled Celeste and she whirled around to see her grandmother—or rather her grandmother's ghost—standing on the other side of the room.

"Gram!" Celeste's breath rushed out. Her grandmother's ghost had a habit of popping up when Celeste was deep in thought. You'd think she'd be used to it by now. "You scared me."

Her grandmother laughed. "They teach us that over here, you know. Ghosts are supposed to scare people."

Celeste frowned. "Really?"

"Nah, I just do it because it's fun." Grandma's ghost cocked her head to the side as if listening. "What the heck is going on here? Are you guys opening a bed and breakfast?"

Celeste laughed. "No. We're just having some guests."

Grandma nodded. "I heard you guys had some goings on. In fact, that's why I'm here."

Celeste's brows shot up. "Really. You mean you can help us?"

"Maybe. I had a visit from Ezra Finch. You know, I knew him back in the day. Of course, he was quite old back in my day, but we used to all go to him for his remedies."

Celeste nodded. "Oh."

"Well, anyway, the guy always did think he was the cat's meow. But he said he had an important message for you so here I am."

Celeste leaned forward. "What's the message?"

Grandma's ghost swirled over to the window. She lifted her semi-translucent arm and pushed the curtain aside. "Lovely day today."

Celeste gritted her teeth. One thing she'd learned about Grandma's ghost was that she loved to play up the big moment. She was stretching it out, making Celeste wait.

"The message?" Celeste prompted.

"Oh. Right." The ghost turned from the window, her forehead creasing. "He was very cryptic. Of course, he was that way in life, too. Anyway, he said you made a grave mistake."

Celeste frowned. "No kidding. We misinterpreted the clues. That's not a very helpful message. Are you sure that's what he said?"

"Yes, but I felt like he meant it in a literal way. Not that you just made a mistake. If you get my

165

drift." Gram's ghost drifted up and down to stress the last word.

Celeste chewed her bottom lip. More literal? What did that mean? And then it clicked in.

"That's it!" She rushed over to Gram's ghost and attempted a hug which only resulted in her feeling wet, cold and a little queasy. "Thanks! I know exactly what he meant."

She brushed water vapor off her arms and rushed from the room.

***

Celeste took the front stairs two at a time, arriving in the foyer just as Morgan and Fiona were coming in the front door.

"I know what we did wrong!" Celeste said, then frowned at Fiona when she noticed Belladonna curled up in her arms. "What were you doing with the cat?"

"She must have hidden in the car again." Fiona dumped the cat unceremoniously on the floor. "She was at *Sticks and Stones*."

"What did you mean when you said you knew what we did wrong?" Morgan ignored the cat, who flipped her tail up at them as she slunk away.

"I had a visit from Gram and she gave me a message from Ezra." Celeste continued down the stairs to the oak floor of the foyer. "He said we made a grave mistake."

Morgan made a face. "He said that before, didn't he?"

Fiona shrugged out of her jacket. "And I think Thaddeus said something like that, too."

"Yes, but didn't you think he was using the word 'grave' as an adjective? I know I did. But I think he was really using it as a noun. We made a mistake interpreting the *grave*stone."

"Yeah, no kidding," Jolene said from the top of the stairs where she was carefully helping Johanna down.

Celeste ignored her sister's sarcastic remark and grabbed her cell phone from the foyer table. "The meaning of the epitaph isn't what we thought. We need to look at that again." Her fingers tapped on the screen. "I'll get Cal over here. He's good at this stuff."

"Maybe I can help" Swain appeared at the top of the stairs behind Johanna and Jolene.

"Sure, we can use all the help we can get." Morgan hung her coat on the hall tree. "Let's go to the kitchen."

"Good thing we have a big kitchen," Jolene muttered. She helped Johanna to the last step and then reached for the wheelchair.

"Can't you see that I can walk?" Johanna pushed her away. "I came down the stairs, didn't I?"

"With my help..."

"Fine, then you can help me *walk* into the kitchen."

Celeste, Morgan and Fiona went ahead, leaving their sister and mother to battle their way into the kitchen behind them. Celeste filled the Keurig with water and turned it on. Her phone pinged.

"Cal's just down the street. He'll be here in five."

Cal arrived just as they were all settled in, with coffees in hand. His brows raised up when he noticed Johanna seated in one of the tall kitchen bar stools instead of the wheelchair he was accustomed to seeing her in.

She beamed at his unspoken question. "I'm walking much better now ... though I guess I'll still need the chair a bit."

"That's great." He made his way over to Celeste and planted a kiss on her cheek, causing a flurry of butterflies in her stomach. She looked up at him and time paused as they smiled into each other's eyes. They'd been a couple now for almost two years, but he still made her heart beat faster every time she saw him.

"Enough with the lovey-dovey stuff," Jolene said. "Let's get down to business."

Cal flushed and Celeste cleared her throat, then put a piece of lined paper on the kitchen island. "I wrote the epitaph down on here ... of course we still don't know the bottom line." She avoided looking at Jolene. She knew her sister was already down in the dumps about the loss of her paranormal gifts and she didn't want to make her feel worse by reminding her that her photographic memory would really help them out now.

"Let me see," Cal angled it toward him. "We already have the clue that the relic is a mortar and pestle ... that must be what he means by 'when two become one'."

"Good thinking. The mortar and pestle combine into one item that makes the remedies!" Swain said. "So the rest of that line, 'the healing's begun' makes perfect sense."

"Right." Cal nodded. "We thought the second line was linked to the first and it might still be. At first, we assumed the first line referred to Ezra and Lila-Mae becoming one in marriage, so we assumed the second line referred to where they became one. The church."

"But, that was wrong and if we follow the same logic, 'My favorite place under the sun' would be where the mortar and pestle come together," Swain added.

"His pharmacy on the Finch farm." Celeste's heart plummeted in her chest. "But it burned down years ago. We'll never find the relic there now."

Cal held up his hand. "Let's just get through the rest of the epitaph before we lose hope. There might be another clue that will help."

"The next line, 'look to the west, I can finally rest', looks like a clue that the relic can be found in the western section of the shop," Swain said.

"Which doesn't help us now that the pharmacy is no longer there," Jolene said without looking up from the piece of paper she was scribbling on.

"The building itself isn't there. But didn't you girls say there was still some debris?" Johanna asked.

Fiona nodded. "You don't think the mortar and pestle could still be there in the remains?"

Johanna shrugged. "You never know."

"What's that last part, 'I can finally rest', mean?" Celeste asked.

"Probably once he'd hidden the relic and written the clue, he felt like he could finally rest. His job was done and he could go to his grave in peace," Cal answered.

Celeste sighed. "None of that is very helpful."

"No, but at lest it gives us someplace new to look. The mortar and pestle was hidden in the pharmacy. We just have to figure out what happened to it after the fire," Morgan pointed out.

"I hope it wasn't made out of wood," Fiona said.

Celeste grimaced. "Yeah, it could have burned and not even exist anymore."

Swain's face clouded over. "No. I refuse to think that. We don't know what it was made out of, so let's not assume. It could have been metal, or alabaster or even cement." He glanced at the ceiling. "Mother needs that mortar and pestle desperately."

Celeste's heart pinched. She hoped they could find it for Swain's sake in addition to the real reason—to keep it out of the hands of Bly or anyone else who would use it for bad intent. "We need to narrow down exactly what it was made out of and if it had any distinguishing marks. It's not like mortar and pestles are rare and we can't test out every one of them we see by compounding remedies and seeing how well they work."

"Well, the last line probably gives you a clue to that," Cal said.

Jolene pushed the piece of paper she'd been writing on into the middle of the island. Celeste could see that it had a series of lines and curved semicircles.

"I've started to remember a little of it." Jolene pointed to the symbols. "That's the beginning of the line. At least, I think it is."

Cal swung the paper to face him and squinted at it. "That's a good start. I can already tell by the tops of the letters that the first word is probably 'It's'."

Celeste angled her head to look at the paper straight on like Cal was. Now that he'd said it, she could clearly see he was right about what the first word was. Excitement built in her chest. "What about the others? Can you tell what they are?"

Cal pressed his lips together. "Not with any degree of certainty. I think the next word could be 'the'. It makes sense with the first word. But that next word is harder. See how it has a curved top? It could start with a 'B' or a 'P' or even a 'C'. It's impossible to tell until you fill in some of the other letters and words."

"So it's kind of like *Wheel of Fortune* or something?" Morgan asked. "You have to piece together what it could be based on the other letters that you know for sure."

Cal laughed. "Yes, very much like that. As long as the tops of the letters really are what was on there. Otherwise, you might end up going down a rabbit hole."

Everyone looked at Jolene.

Jolene's face was grim. "I *think* they are right. I can't say for sure. I'm all screwed up and not very much help at all, I'm afraid."

Celeste's heart pinched. "Maybe what we find out from Finch will help us piece it together."

Swain's mouth tightened. "If your friend Bly was the one behind the gravestone smashing, then he probably knows what that last line is."

"And he could be figuring out where the relic is right now," Fiona added.

"We better get a move-on, then." Morgan pushed up from her chair and headed toward the hall.

"Where are we going?" Jolene followed close on her heels.

"To see the only other person who might remember what that last line is," Morgan said without breaking stride. "Thaddeus Finch."

Chapter Seventeen

"So, where are the amulets?" Celeste asked as they drove down Shore Road on their way to the nursing home.

"They're at the shop," Fiona replied from the back seat where she was twisted around, inspecting the cargo area of the TrailBlazer. "I wanted to make sure the solder was cooled completely before we wore them so I left them there. We can pick them up after we talk to Finch."

"I'm a little worried about trusting Finch's information," Morgan said. "It might not be reliable. You heard what Wendy said in the shop, and she would know more than anyone about his mental acuity."

"Wendy?" Jolene had taken the piece of paper with the tops of the letters with her and had been scribbling on it as they drove. "Finch's health aide?"

"Yes." Fiona turned forward in her seat and then bent down to look under the passenger seat.

"She was at your shop?"

"Yeah, I guess Finch told her about it," Morgan said.

Jolene paused, her pencil over the paper. "Well, she believed him when he told her you had a shop, so he can't be *that* unreliable."

"Good point." Fiona's muffled voice came from the floor where she was crouched down, looking underneath her own seat.

"What are you looking for?" Celeste asked.

"Belladonna. She keeps showing up and I just know she is stowing away in the car somewhere."

"Probably. She's pretty sneaky," Celeste said. "But if she doesn't want to be found, you won't find her. Besides, she can take care of herself."

"Yeah, but I don't want her to suddenly show up inside the nursing home." Fiona settled back in her seat just as Morgan pulled into a parking spot.

"Now that we know the relic is a mortar and pestle, the fact that those very items were stolen from the Oblate Museum makes me think the paranormal mortar and pestle might have been there the whole time," Celeste said as their feet crunched across the icy parking lot snow.

"I was thinking the same thing," Morgan replied. "Except Dorian said that she knew for sure that the bad guys didn't have the relic after the museum break-in."

"True." Celeste opened the nursing home door and the nurse waved them through.

"We'll ask Finch," Fiona said. "Maybe he can clear it up."

They got to Finch's door and Jolene's heart tugged at the sight of the old man lying in bed, his face a sickly, waxen yellow. He looked old and frail. Her questioning eyes met Wendy's.

"He's not doing well today," Wendy said.

"Oh, what's wrong?" Jolene asked.

Wendy shrugged. "Maybe he's just tired. You shouldn't plan to stay long."

"Stay schmay." Finch raised himself up to a sitting position, seeming to perk up a little. "They can stay as long as they want."

Wendy held a small paper cup out to Finch. "Whatever you like, Mr. Finch. Just take this pill first. You need your rest."

Wendy leaned across Finch and Jolene caught sight of a black pendant dangling down from her neck. She glanced at Fiona, assuming it was the one Wendy had purchased earlier. Wendy saw her looking and curled her fist around the pendant.

"Do you like the necklace?" Fiona asked.

"Yes, it's very nice," Wendy answered.

"Oh, do you know each other?" Finch asked.

"We met her here the other day," Fiona reminded him. "And then Wendy came to our shop and bought the necklace. Thanks for telling her about our shop, by the way."

"You girls have a shop?" Finch's brows mashed together and he looked from one Blackmoore to the other in confusion.

"Yes, remember you told me about it." Wendy raised her brows at the sisters and mouthed the words. "He's not very lucid today."

Finch tipped back the cup that held his pill, then shoved it out at Wendy. "Here. Take this. I'm going to talk to my friends."

Wendy took the empty cup, then sidled her way past the girls. "I'll be back in a few minutes. Don't stay too long." She glanced back at Finch, her face pinched with concern. "I don't know how much energy he has left."

A rock lodged in the pit of Jolene's stomach. It seemed like Finch had gone downhill quickly and she was kind of starting to like the old guy. She hoped he would be okay.

Morgan launched right into a line of questioning. "Hey, Mr. Finch. Do you remember your great-grandfather's pharmacy?"

His face brightened. "Do I ever!"

"After he died, what happened to it?"

"We kept it the way he always had it. He instructed us to do that in his will, you know."

"You didn't donate anything to the museum in town?" Fiona asked.

Finch pursed his lips together and squinted his eyes shut. He was silent for a long time. So long that Jolene feared he might not ever answer. If it wasn't for his contorted face, she might have even thought he was no longer with them. Then he blurted out, "No. We didn't donate anything from the pharmacy. It had already burned down."

"So, what happened to the contents after the fire?" Morgan asked.

"The police took it as evidence." Finch leaned forward and gestured for the girls to come closer to the bed. "The fire was suspicious, you know."

"We didn't know." Jolene glanced at her sisters. Could the fire have been set years ago to get at the relic? If so, whoever did it had apparently been unsuccessful.

"So nothing was left from the pharmacy after the fire?" Morgan asked.

"Well, there were a few things. I went out there when my arthritis wasn't acting up and dug a couple old bottles out, but most anything that was any good was carted off to the police station." Finch screwed his face up. "Come to think of it, I never saw any of that stuff again."

Celeste tilted her head to the left and looked at Finch. "If most everything was at the police station, what items did you donate to the museum?"

"Oh, that was just some old memorabilia we had in the attic. My great-grandfather had a lot of stuff and my grand-pappy saved newspaper articles about him in the attic," Finch said. "When the museum came looking for donations, that's what I gave them."

Jolene felt a spark of hope. "Were the items from the attic Ezra's most special items?"

"Oh, no. He kept the good stuff in his pharmacy building."

Morgan looked skeptical. "And your family kept everything in there even long after he was dead?"

"Yes! Grandpappy insisted we leave it as is. No one would dare go against Ezra, even if he was six feet under," Finch said. "He fancied it to be a museum of sorts. Especially that back wall. The one opposite the ocean. That's where he had his collection of antique equipment."

Jolene looked sharply at her sisters. "You mean the wall on the west side."

Finch gave her a sour look. "Well, unless things have changed, the wall opposite the ocean would be on the west side. We never touched a thing in there. Left it just as it was on his last day. But then it burned down, so I guess nothing lasts forever."

"Was there anything that your great-grandfather liked in particular? A mortar and pestle that was special to him or his favorite, perhaps?" Morgan ventured.

"Morty Postner?" Finch nodded excitedly. "Yes, he played cards with my great-granddaddy. I don't think he was anything special though. Is it important?"

The girls exchange an exasperated look. Celeste tried another tactic. "Do you remember much from when your great-grandfather died?"

Finch settled back into the pillows, his small body all but disappearing in the bed. He looked so frail and sickly that Jolene wondered if he had the energy to answer. Then a smile crossed his face and he appeared to rally.

"He was quite old when he died. Almost one hundred, but still, it was quite a blow to the household. Daddy was right upset and I think I remember him complaining about some oddities in great-grandpa's will. You know, like keeping the pharmacy open as a museum of sorts. Daddy didn't want to have to deal with that."

Fiona's brows mashed together. "Come to think of it, I don't remember ever visiting a museum on your farm."

"It wasn't open to the public," Finch said. "I remember my parents saying something about liability and they didn't want strangers on the farmland, so they abided by his will as best they could by keeping everything set up as it was the day he died. They just didn't let the public come in and view it." A smile crossed his face. "It sure was a fun place to go and play as a kid. I had to sneak in, of course. Momma didn't want me to go in there."

"Do you remember anything special in there?" Celeste asked. "An item you were drawn to more so than the others?"

"I don't remember much except the night I stole a kiss from Sue Ellen Mayfair next to the apothecary cabinet. That old pharmacy building sure was a good place to take the girls," he chuckled.

Jolene grimaced. She didn't want to listen to tales of Finch's adolescent exploits, so she changed the subject. "When we were at the graveyard, we noticed Ezra had an interesting epitaph on his gravestone. Do you know anything about that?"

Finch's mouth twisted to the left. "I remember that was another bone of contention with my parents. Ezra wanted a particular poem on there and Mama said it was dumb. But he had it in his will and no one wanted to go against him."

"I thought the poem was lovely," Morgan lied. "It was something like 'When two become one, the healing's begun, in my favorite place under the sun. Look to the west, I can finally rest ...' Do you remember it?"

Finch nodded. "Yes ... yes, I think I do. But wasn't there something else?"

"Yes, there's a last line." Morgan's eyes drilled into his. "Do you remember what it is?"

Finch puffed out his cheeks. "Now, you'd think I would. As a little kid I spent a lot of time there in that graveyard. It seemed so peaceful, almost as if my great-granddaddy was there with me." Jolene's eyes meet Celeste's over the bed. Little did Finch know Ezra probably really was with him in that graveyard.

"Anyway, I think it was something about someone being pretty," Finch continued.

Jolene took the piece of paper she'd been working on the whole time over to Finch's bed and sat on the side facing him. She showed it to him. "Maybe you can help us figure it out. I've got some of the letters written here. Maybe these letters will help you fill in the rest of the line, just like they do on *Wheel of Fortune*."

Finch perked up. "I love *Wheel of Fortune*!" He lifted his head to look at the paper in Jolene's hands. "Let's see. The beginning is already filled in. 'It's the' ... but I think something is screwed up. It looks like there's more 'e's that didn't get filled in. Whoever bought that vowel got ripped off. Look, they should go here, here, here, and here. Some doubles, too."

Finch pointed to several places on the paper where there were small arcs, like the top of the lowercase letter 'e'. Jolene filled them in tentatively. She doubted he was right, but she figured there was no harm in testing it out.

Finch stared at the letters. "Now, let me see. Is there an 'N'?"

Jolene shrugged. "I don't think so."

"Yes. Right here and here." Finch pointed at two more spots and Jolene filled them with 'n's.

Finch laid back in the bed, a satisfied look on his face. "Yes! I'll solve the puzzle. The phrase is 'It's the prettiest green you've ever seen!' That's what my great-granddaddy had on his gravestone!"

Chapter Eighteen

"The prettiest green you've ever seen? What the heck does that mean?" Celeste asked once they were in the car on their way to *Sticks and Stones*.

"Who knows," Fiona answered. "Could a mortar and pestle be green? None of Morgan's are."

Morgan's lips pressed in a thin line. "Most modern ones are made of porcelain or brass. Some older ones could be wood. I have seen ones made out of glass but those aren't practical, for obvious reasons."

"But this one is magic," Jolene cut in. "So maybe it could have been made out of glass. Green glass. I'll text Brody and see if we can get a list of items that the police have from the pharmacy. Maybe we'll luck out and he'll have a green mortar and pestle."

"It could also be copper that turns green with age." Fiona twisted in her seat to look out the back window.

"That's possible. It *was* ancient." Morgan angled the rear-view mirror to look at Fiona, then asked, "Are you looking for Belladonna again?"

"No, I thought I saw someone following us. A black car." Fiona twisted back to face front. "It was probably my imagination. I'll feel better once we get to the shop and pick up the amulets."

"I noticed the necklace Wendy bought from you was obsidian," Jolene said. "It was a lot like our amulets."

"Yes, but that's not one of the protective amulets. That stone wasn't infused with special energy like ours."

"Oh. Well, that's good." Jolene, in the passenger seat, glanced in the side view mirror. Was that a black car way back? Was it following them? No. Fiona was making her paranoid. She looked down at the piece of paper in her hand, then held it up. "Do you think this is really what the last line of the gravestone said?"

"It fits." Morgan slid her eyes over to Jolene. "*If* the marks you made are actually what was on there, those letters would line up."

"It might not have anything to do with the mortar and pestle, though," Fiona said. "Maybe he really was talking about Lila-Mae's eyes."

"The prettiest green?" Jolene tapped the paper with the eraser end of her pencil. "It could be, but that brings us back to our original assumption that the whole poem was about him and Lila-Mae, and when we assumed that before, we were told we made a grave mistake."

"Plus those clues led us to dead ends," Celeste added.

"Well, I don't know. A green mortar and pestle is kind of odd, but green eyes are not," Fiona said.

Something niggled in Jolene's memory. Could it be that the last line really was about Lila-Mae's eyes? It made more sense, but she knew it couldn't be right. She sat back into the seat while the gears in her brain ground slowly, and then she remembered why it couldn't be about her eyes. She sat up excitedly—maybe her memory skills *were* coming back. "I remember on one of our other visits, Finch said Lila-Mae had eyes like Wendy, and her eyes are gray. So it couldn't have been about Lila-Mae's eyes."

"Unless Finch wasn't having a lucid moment when he said that," Celeste suggested.

Morgan pulled up at *Sticks and Stones* and they all got out. Fiona glanced back over her shoulder as they piled onto the front porch while Morgan unlocked the door.

"I don't see that we have much else to go on." Morgan pushed the door open. "So let's assume the last line is about the mortar and pestle."

"At least a green one will be easy to find." Fiona gestured for Celeste and Jolene to precede her inside, cast one last glance down the road, then closed the door behind them.

Jolene felt an immediate rush of energy, just like she did every time she came into the shop. There was something about it that unnerved her

187

and empowered her at the same time. The shop was special, but she really didn't know why.

They followed Fiona to her work area. She picked up four necklaces, handing them out to each of the girls. Jolene slipped hers on her neck and immediately felt calmer. The obsidian amulet would help bounce off any negative energy that got directed toward her, but only if she got the stone directly in the stream of the energy. With her skills not functioning properly, she could use all the help she could get. The necklaces, along with the mica mirror they'd borrowed from Swain, would give them an edge if they were attacked.

"If we're going to the pharmacy ruins, we should have brought that mica mirror," Jolene said.

"I actually did." Fiona smiled. "It's in a box in the back of the car."

"That box?" Celeste frowned. I moved that because it was bouncing around and it seemed kind of heavy for the—"

"*Meow!*"

Jolene whirled toward the sound. Belladonna sat by the door, eyeing them with her ice-blue eyes. She flicked her tail, then trotted toward the front of the room. "Hey, I thought you took her home."

"I did!" Fiona narrowed her eyes at the cat.

"Yeah, I saw you," Celeste said. "You dropped her off in the foyer."

"And now she's back." Morgan crossed her arms over her chest. "I wonder if she was hiding out in that box."

"It was kind of heavy," Celeste said. "But even if she was ... how did she get in here? She didn't come in with us and the door has been closed the whole time."

"*Merrrrow!*" Belladonna sprang up as if she knew she was being discussed. She raced around the edge of the room, leaping into the air and batting at invisible foes.

"She did that this morning, too," Fiona said. "And she batted one of my earrings into the crack under the wall ... right where she is now."

Jolene watched the cat as she snaked one slim white paw under the crack in the wall, twisting and turning as if she was prying something out. And then, with a shriek, she whipped her paw out, sending a small object spinning into the center of the room.

"My earring!" Fiona stomped over to the object, stopped it's rotation with her foot, then picked it up.

"I don't know what gets into her," Morgan said.

"Me, either." Fiona held the earring up. It was an intense, emerald green color with black lines that glowed in the bright morning light from the window.

"What's that made of?" Morgan asked.

"Malachite." Fiona angled it and the light shone through the center, giving it a nearly translucent green glow. "Isn't it pretty?"

"It's gorgeous. What an amazing green," Morgan said.

"Yep. It's one of my favorites." Fiona palmed the earring and headed toward the case.

"Wait a minute!" Jolene felt the hairs on her arm raise. "It's green. It's the prettiest green I've ever seen!"

The sisters stared at each other with wide eyes.

"The mortar and pestle isn't glass or brass, it's malachite!" Celeste said.

"That makes perfect sense," Morgan said excitedly. "Malachite is a stone, so it could easily be imbued with powerful healing properties, just like the obsidian amulets or Fiona's carnelians."

Jolene pulled out her cell phone and checked her email. "Brody sent me the lists from the museum theft and the fire." She opened the email and downloaded the two attachments, then opened the first one. "All the mortar and pestles stolen from the museum were wooden. There's nothing green."

"Maybe it's at the police station," Morgan said.

"That would be convenient." Celeste picked up Belladonna, who seemed unusually willing to be held.

Jolene opened the second attachment. "Oh, good, these are all categorized. Let me look under the mortars category. Let's see … cherry wood, cast iron, porcelain, marble, stoneware." Jolene looked up at her sisters. "Nothing green."

Morgan pursed her lips. "If it wasn't stolen from the museum and it's not at the police station, there's only one other place it could be."

"The rubble from the pharmacy on the Finch farm."

Chapter Nineteen

Jolene pulled the door open, letting a gust of cold wind into the shop. "Come on. Let's get out to the farm—we don't have any time to waste!"

"Whoa." Morgan held up her palms. "Let's think this through. We don't want to just run around like chickens with our heads cut off."

"Right," Fiona agreed. "If we're going to go dig in the pharmacy, we should get Swain. He can organize it to make sure we cover every inch."

"Plus we need to drop someone off." Morgan tilted her head toward Belladonna, who was purring contentedly in Celeste's arms.

Jolene sighed and closed the door. "Okay, fine. But let's hurry. We don't want Bly ... or anyone else to get a jump on us!"

It was only a short ride to the Blackmoore home from the shop. Jolene couldn't help but notice Morgan's periodic uneasy glances at the side-view mirror.

They parked in the driveway and Celeste got out first, still carrying Belladonna, with Fiona following right behind her. Jolene pulled Morgan back a few steps.

"Is something wrong?"

"No." Morgan glanced back behind them. "I mean, I don't think so. I'm not sure, but I feel a bit uneasy. The faster we get digging and recover the relic, the better."

No kidding. That's what I was trying to say at the shop, Jolene thought as she followed Morgan inside.

"Up here." Celeste poked her head over the railing from upstairs. Jolene went up, following the sounds of voices to a room at the end of the hall—the one she'd helped Johanna set up for Swain's mother.

She peeked in cautiously, her heart leaping into her throat at the sight of the sallow, shrunken woman in the bed.

"Is ... is she okay?" Jolene ventured.

Swain chewed his bottom lip, which Jolene noticed was raw. His face looked wan, his tan seeming to have faded overnight.

"She's holding her own," Johanna said from the head of the bed, where she was holding a spoonful of something goopy to the woman's lips. "Annabella, these are my daughters."

The woman's eyes fluttered open. They were sunken and hazy, but Jolene could see a tiny spark inside. A will to live. Her heart fluttered— they *had* to help this woman and give her a chance to get better.

"Hi, there. Your momma and Gunner told me what's going on. It sure is nice of you girls to go to all this trouble to help me. I don't know how I could ever repay you." Her voice was weak, barely a whisper.

"Oh, shush. No repayment necessary," Johanna said.

"Well, you people must be magic," Annabella said," I haven't felt like eating in days, but this stuff you're feeding me is giving me my appetite back."

"That's Mateo." Johanna winked at Jolene, then looked back at Annabella. "He cooked up something special for you."

Jolene's brows pulled into a tight 'V'. "Mateo's here?"

"He's downstairs in the kitchen." Johanna nodded toward the stairs. "Why don't you go see what he's cooking up?"

"Yeah, I should do that." Jolene followed the smell of ginger and cinnamon to the kitchen, where Mateo stood at the stove. He didn't see her at first and she paused in the doorway, wondering why his broad shoulders and dark, curly hair made her heart flutter.

"Hi," she said finally.

He turned, looking at her with velvety, brown eyes. A smile spread across his face. The contrast of his pearly white teeth against dark skin seemed to light up the room.

What is it with this guy? Jolene wondered, then gave herself a mental head shake. The last thing she needed was to get all woozy over a guy ... especially one that can't be relied upon to stick around.

"What are you cooking?" she asked.

"Oh, just something my grandmother used to make for me when I was sick." He wiped his hand on the black apron he had tied around his slim hips. "How is the search going?"

Mateo's brows climbed up his forehead as Jolene told him how they'd figured out the relic was a mortar and pestle and their theory that it might still be buried in the remains of the burned-out pharmacy.

"That sounds promising." Has face turned thoughtful. "You better be careful, though. Bly's guys are in town."

"The bearded guys?"

"Yep."

"Well, they already attacked us and we kicked their butts." Jolene said proudly. "Though that was before I got clonked with that tree and lost my powers." Jolene's stomach constricted and she looked down at her hand. *Would she ever regain her special gift?*

Mateo's face creased with concern. "Have you regained any of your gifts?"

Jolene's heart skipped. She didn't know if it was because of the look on Mateo's face or

195

because she was just as worried as he was about the loss of her paranormal gifts.

She sucked in a deep breath. "I think so ... at least my memory seems to be better." She motioned for him to step aside. "Stand back."

Jolene closed her eyes and flexed her fingers. Then she pointed toward the kitchen door. She focused on her energy. Concentrating. Straining. And then she felt it ... a little tingle at her fingertips. Not as strong as the feeling she usually got, but it was something. She pushed the energy out and then stared down at her fingers as a small blob of greenish-blue energy dribbled out and plopped onto the floor. She watched in disappointment as the ineffective blob shriveled up and disappeared.

Tears prick the backs of her eyes. "I guess my command of energy isn't coming back as good as my memory."

Mateo took her hand in his and looked deep into her eyes. "Don't worry ... it will come back. You have to believe that it will."

She looked down at her tiny, pale hand in his large, tanned one. Would it come back? Of all the sisters, she had the most powerful defensive skills. Her sisters were counting on her to use her gifts to fight off Bly's minions, but what if she couldn't come through for them?

"Ahem." Morgan cleared her throat from the doorway, where she stood holding up a burlap bag. "Swain gave us these tools for the dig. He's meeting us after his mom is done eating. Let's get a move on ... we have to get to that pharmacy before Bly figures out the same thing and beats us to it!"

Chapter Twenty

Fiona followed her sisters across the barren landscape of the Finch farm's front yard. In the distance, a pile of rubble and black boards stuck out of the snow. She pulled her scarf tight around her neck and flexed her fingers inside her gloves, glad that she'd worn her warmest pair.

The pharmacy hadn't been big—about ten feet by fifteen. Thankfully, they didn't have a lot of ground to cover.

"So what do we do?" Celeste surveyed the area. "Lay it out in grids or something? Did Swain give you any instructions?"

Morgan shook her head, then glanced back over the yard toward the road. "He should be here soon."

"Well, I'm not going to just stand here and wait for him." Jolene stomped her feet to increase circulation. "It's too cold out here. Let's start digging."

"Where do we start?" Fiona asked.

"In the west, of course." Jolene headed to what would have been the west wall of the pharmacy and jumped down into the depression in the ground.

Fiona followed her, her heart sinking when she saw what a mess it was. "All I see is a pile of dirt, rocks and burned wood."

"Well, the police did take most of it, but since we are actually looking for a rock, I think we better start sifting." Jolene was already on her hands and knees, picking up rocks and tossing them aside along with charred timbers. Fiona noticed Jolene's hands were filthy, but her black parka didn't show any dirt.

She looked down at her own purple jacket and grimaced. Wishing she had been smart enough to wear black, too, she climbed down into the hole next to Jolene and got to work.

Morgan's phone chirped. She looked at the display and swore under her breath. "It's Luke."

"So, don't answer," Jolene shot over her shoulder.

"He'll just keep calling if I don't." Morgan sighed and put the phone up to her ear. "Hello? ... Who told you that? .... Swain, oh, yeah, well we are here, but ...—" Morgan held the phone out from her ear and Fiona could hear Luke yelling through it.

"Fine. Send Gordy and the guys, but I'm pretty sure we weren't followed." Morgan's eyes drifted across the field to the road.

Fiona followed her gaze, but she couldn't see the road. She remembered the black truck that had been following them earlier. Were Bly's paranormals out there somewhere, waiting to attack? It was probably a good thing to have Luke's guys watching over them just in case.

Fiona turned back to her digging and Morgan's conversation with Luke faded into the background. She shoved a timber aside and a portion of it flaked off, disintegrating in a puff of black soot and spicing the air with the smell of charcoal. Her fingers grew cold despite the heavy duty gloves, and she pulled one glove off to blow warm air on the tips.

She eyed the stones in the rubble. Picking a few up, she hefted them in her hand, feeling their weight.

Would she ever be able to use them as weapons?

She glanced at Jolene ... what if her sister never recovered? She'd have to do something to fill the hole in their defenses.

She clenched her fist. The jagged edges of the rocks cut into her palm. She could feel the rocks getting warmer. Did she dare open her hand? Did she dare believe in her paranormal abilities? She brought her hand up, the fist still clenched. Her fingers started to curl open—

"Hey, look at this!" Jolene's excitement-tinged voice diverted Fiona's focus. Her hand opened and she dropped the stones into her pocket while she scurried to Jolene's side.

Jolene was standing over a shallow hole she'd excavated, holding a big rock in her hand. It was covered in soot, looking just like every other rock out there.

"It's just a rock." Celeste came up behind her and looked over her shoulder.

"I don't think so. Look at this." Jolene brushed away some of the soot and Fiona could see the rock was tinged with green. Then Jolene turned it over to reveal the other side, which was smoothly polished with a deep well in the center. Deep enough to be used as a mortar.

Morgan gasped and reached out for the rock. Jolene handed it over and Morgan held it in her right hand, rubbing the smooth surface with her fingertips. The polished side was beautiful swirls of green with some black mixed in.

"This is it." Morgan stared down at the rock. "It's the mortar ... the relic."

"No wonder the police missed it. It just looks like a rock," Celeste said.

"Yeah, especially on the unpolished side. It was lying face down, wedged in between two boards." Jolene's voice was edged with wonder. "And it's been sitting out here the whole time."

"But where's the pestle?" Morgan asked.

They all looked at Jolene, who glanced down at the hole. "I didn't find one."

"Well, it's got to be here." Morgan crouched down and started sifting through the dirt. Fiona and Celeste followed suit.

One hour later, Gordy and two of Luke's guys had come to 'guard' them and been put to work, but no pestle was found.

"There's got to be one." Morgan threw down a rock she'd picked up thinking it might be the pestle. "The mortar is no good without it."

"Right. 'When two become one, the healing's begun'." Jolene quoted the epitaph. "It won't work unless the remedy is made with the mortar and pestle together."

"Well, it's not here." Fiona brushed dirt and soot off her hands. "We've looked through the whole thing."

"Maybe we didn't do it methodically enough." Morgan glanced out at the road. "Where is Swain? He should be here helping."

Fiona stepped back up onto level ground and surveyed the rubble. "It shouldn't be hard to find because of the shape. It wouldn't look like a rock like the mortar did. It would be shaped and polished. You'd think it would stick out like a sore thumb."

"Well, if it would stick out for us, then it would stick out for anyone." Jolene pulled her phone out and started tapping on the screen. "The list of items taken from the pharmacy fire is categorized.

I didn't see the mortar and pestle, but if the pestle was found by itself … Yes! Here it is under miscellaneous. Rounded green scepter—possibly some kind of polished rock—five inches long.

"That sounds like it! That's the length it should be." Morgan said. "They must not have realized it was a pestle because they didn't find the matching mortar."

"So, it's at the police station?" Celeste asked.

Jolene shrugged. "It seems that way."

Morgan tucked the mortar in the crook of her arm and turned toward the car. "Then, what are we waiting for? Let's go get it!"

Chapter Twenty-One

The inside of the Noquitt police station was quiet, which wasn't unusual seeing as there wasn't much crime in Noquitt, especially in the off-season. Morgan had given the mortar to Gordy and had instructed him and the guys to meet them back at the Blackmoore house after promising they would head there themselves just as soon as they got a look at the pestle. Jolene didn't think Brody would let them take it—they'd probably have to resort to other means to get it in their possession once they verified it really was part of the relic.

"This is from years ago. I don't know..." Brody gave the girls a sideways glance. "The evidence room is pretty disorganized and this must be way in the back."

"Surely no one will mind if you just bring it out for us to look at?" Jolene leaned her upper half over the counter that served as a receptionist desk to look in at the rest of the station. "It looks like no one is even here."

Brody glanced behind him. "I'm not sure if I should..."

"Is there some official request form?" Jolene whipped out her cell phone. "I'll text Jake and see if he can get something official filled out."

"And if that doesn't work, I'll have Luke get it through his government contact," Morgan said importantly.

Brody's eyes narrowed at the mention of his older brother. He knew Luke worked for a clandestine government agency, and Jolene could tell he didn't want to get on the wrong side of his brother or the government. "Well, okay. I guess it won't hurt to let you guys have a look." He turned and headed toward the door that led to the back of the police station. "You guys stay out here."

Morgan's face registered disappointment at being left in the lobby, but they stood out there dutifully as he disappeared into the inner sanctum of the police department.

Fiona and Celeste sat in the orange plastic chairs that lined one wall. Morgan paced in front of the door and Jolene tapped her fingers impatiently on the counter while they waited a long twenty minutes for Brody to return.

Just when Jolene thought he'd forgotten about them, the door opened and Brody appeared. His face was red and a bead of sweat clung to his upper lip.

"Brody, what's wrong?" Morgan asked.

"That item you were looking for..." He looked down at the floor, a mixture of concern and embarrassment spreading on his face. "It's missing."

Morgan shot Brody an incredulous look. "What do you mean missing?"

"Well, it *was* here." He ducked back behind the door and pulled out a box with a loose leaf notebook on top. He opened the notebook to a page of photos and pointed to one in the middle. It was obviously a malachite pestle. *The* pestle. The second half of the relic. "This is it, right?"

Morgan nodded. "Yes, it looks like it."

"As you can see, all the items were photographed and catalogued." Brody pointed to the loose leaf notebook with the photos in it. "So it *was* here. But when I looked for it out back, I couldn't find it."

"Are you sure, maybe you missed it? Its not that big." Celeste suggested.

Brody pushed the big box toward them. "Look for yourself. These are the only items back there from the Finch case."

Jolene frowned at the box. "That doesn't seem like nearly as many as items as were on the list."

"Could some of the items have been filed away somewhere else ... or returned to the family?" Morgan knelt down beside the box and started sifting through the items.

"Anything is possible." He glanced behind him then leaned in toward the sisters and lowered his voice. "The fire happened right as Overton was taking over from the old Sheriff. That was before my time, but I heard things weren't run very well at first and there were a lot of slip-ups. These items might have been a casualty of that. Some of the chain of evidence records seem to be missing, so I can't tell where anything went."

Fiona's lips pressed together. "Why did you need evidence from the fire, anyway?"

"It seems the fire was thought to be suspicious," Brody said. "Near as I can tell, it was eventually ruled an accident. So, by rights, the family could have claimed all this stuff and taken int back. But since the records are all screwed up, I don't know what really happened."

"If the family did take it back, why is this box still here?" Morgan wondered.

Brody shrugged. "Like I said, it seems like things weren't run properly back then, so maybe they didn't give the family everything or maybe the family never got it back and the rest of it got lost somewhere."

Jolene turned to her sisters in frustration. "So, now what?"

Morgan stood up. "Well, It's definitely not in there. I think there's only one hope of finding out where it is. We need to talk to Thaddeus Finch."

Chapter Twenty-Two

Fiona drove the TrailBlazer to the nursing home with Jolene riding shotgun.

"Hey, I have an idea." Jolene fiddled with her phone. "Maybe the pestle *did* get returned to the Finches and it made its way to the museum and then was stolen in the break-in the other day."

"It could be," Celeste said. "I bet Finch would know if it was."

"Even better," Jolene said. "I can just look at the list of items from my email."

"Is it on there?" Celeste asked.

Jolene scanned the list with her finger. "No."

"Oh. Well, at least we still have Finch to talk to." Celeste turned to Morgan. "Shouldn't we tell Luke that we took a detour? He's expecting us to come right home after the police station."

Morgan's lips tightened. "We probably should, but he won't be happy. I turned my phone off at the dig and it won't take long to talk to Finch. I'll turn it on and give him an update when we leave."

Fiona pulled into a parking spot and everyone jumped out. They rushed into the lobby. Fiona started to turn down the hallway that led to Finch's room, but the look on the nurse's face at the receptionist station gave her pause.

"Hi, girls … I'm so sorry for your loss," the nurse said softly.

Fiona's brows snapped together. "Loss? What do you mean?"

The nurse looked startled. "Why, you were friends of Mr. Finch, right?"

"*Were?* Did something happen to him?"

"Oh, dear." The nurse's hands fluttered to her throat. "I thought you knew. "Mr. Finch passed away just over an hour ago."

"What?" Jolene yelled. "He's dead?"

The nurse nodded. "Sorry. I thought you'd already been told and were here to get his things."

"No. We came to talk to him. How could he be dead? We were just here and he seemed okay." Fiona shook her head in disbelief. Sure, Finch had seemed a little under the weather when they were there before, but she didn't think he was only hours from death. "What happened?"

"I don't know. The charge nurse went to check on him and he was no longer with us." The nurse put her hand gently on Fiona's arm. "Don't feel bad, it was his time. He passed peacefully in his sleep, it seems."

"It seems?"

"Well, no one was actually with him, of course, but he was lying in bed and looked peaceful when he was found."

"What about his personal aide?" Jolene asked. "Wasn't she there?"

"Personal aide?" The nurse frowned. "I don't know who you're talking about."

"What was her name?" Morgan screwed up her face. "Wendy! The girl with the long, strawberry blonde hair."

The nurse gave her a puzzled look. "You must be confused. We don't have anyone with long, strawberry blonde hair here and besides, none of the patients have personal aides."

Panic bloomed in Fiona's chest. Wendy was a fraud? If so, who *was* she and why pretend to be Finch's health aide? Did she have something to do with Finch's death? And did *that* have something to do with the pestle? A quick glance at her sisters told her they were asking themselves the same questions.

"Okay, thanks," Morgan said to the nurse, then to her sisters, "Let's go. There's nothing we can do here."

Fiona's shoulders slumped as they walked to the car. "What do we do now?"

"I'm not sure." Morgan got into the driver's seat and the rest of them piled in. "We need to track down this Wendy impostor."

"This is getting weird," Jolene said. "You don't think Finch met with foul play, do you?"

"I don't know," Morgan started the car then sat there worrying her bottom lip as she let the car idle. "It's all very suspicious. What was Wendy doing in Finch's room? And why pretend she was his private aide?"

"And what did she really want when she showed up at our shop?" Fiona added.

"Yeah, that can't be a coincidence," Morgan said. "I just wish—"

"There she is!" Celeste yelled, pointing to a lime green Kia that sped out from behind the building past them, a mane of long, strawberry blonde hair flying out the window.

"Let's follow her!" Jolene shouted. But Morgan didn't need to be told—she'd already jammed the car into gear and had the pedal floored in pursuit.

"Where is she going?" Celeste asked as Morgan dodged Main Street traffic, which was mercifully scant due to it being the off-season.

Looks like she's headed down Thurgood Road," Jolene said.

"I think she's going to the Finch farm," Fiona added.

"Damn it!" Morgan laid on the horn as a tractor pulled out in front of them, slowing them to a crawl.

"What is a tractor doing out in November?" Celeste asked.

"It's Nelson Brown, getting ready for his winter hay rides." Jolene rolled down her window and leaned her upper body out. "Nelson, pull over. We need to get by!"

Nelson pulled to the right and they swerved past him.

"Darn, it's too late. She's gone." Fiona's heart sank. She squinted at the empty road in front of them, searching for a glimpse of the Kia.

"That's okay. I just know that she's going to the Finch farm." Morgan turned down the road that led to the farm. "I feel it in my bones."

She took the road as fast as she could, slowing down only enough to navigate the hairpin turn without going off the road.

"There's her car!" Jolene pointed toward the lime green Kia sitting next to the Finch farm. Morgan pulled in beside it, but it was empty and there was no sign of its driver.

"Where did she go? Is she in the house?" Fiona asked as they piled out of the TrailBlazer and surrounded the Kia.

"It looks like she went this way." Jolene pointed to fresh tracks in the snow that led out across the field toward the cemetery.

"The cemetery?" Morgan started following the tracks. "I guess I shouldn't be surprised."

The snow wasn't very deep, only about an inch, but Fiona was glad she had worn her heavy boots as she jogged up to the graveyard behind her sisters.

As they drew closer to the graveyard, Fiona scanned the outline of the familiar shapes of the stones, looking for the distinctive silhouette of a person, but there was no one to be seen.

"Where is she?" Celeste shaded her eyes with her hand. "Is she hiding behind one of them?"

They mounted the steps to the graveyard and spread out, walking slowly, each of them looking behind the stones.

"Look!" Jolene pointed toward the back of the cemetery where the mausoleum sat, silent and cold, just as it had on their previous trips ... except this time, one of the doors yawned open.

A cold chill skittered up Fiona's spine as she stared at the black interior beyond the door. "Do you think she's in there?"

Morgan shrugged. "I don't know what the heck she would be doing in there, but my gut tells me we better check it out."

"Wait," Jolene cautioned. "She could be leading us on a wild goose chase. She's probably partnered up with Bly. This could be a trap."

Morgan paused. "It could be, but if so, all the more reason to get in there. She knows something about the pestle. I can feel it."

"But we might not be able to defend ourselves..." Jolene looked down at her hands.

"Well, I still have my killer karate moves," Celeste said.

"Plus we have our amulets," Morgan added.

Fiona fingered her amulet. The amulets and mica refractor would help them with the defensive maneuvers of deflecting any energy headed their way, but without Jolene, their hopes of mounting an offensive paranormal attack were nil. And she doubted they could win with only defensive moves.

If only I could get my act together, I might be able to help defend us. Otherwise, we might need help, she thought, then out loud, she said, "Maybe we should tell Luke. He can send the guys to help us out."

Morgan made a face, then turned toward the mausoleum. "There's no time for that. I'm going in."

Chapter Twenty-Three

Fiona stood in the doorway to the mausoleum while her eyes adjusted to the lack of light.

"This is a lot bigger than I thought," Celeste said.

Fiona could see she was right. The room itself was much larger than it appeared from the outside and it looked to have short corridors or niches that sloped downward in all four corners. She wondered how far underground it went ... and hoped they wouldn't have to find out.

"Look!" Jolene pointed to the floor and Fiona recognized a trail of Black Crow licorices.

"Swain?" Morgan's forehead creased. "What is *he* doing here?"

"He double-crossed us!" Jolene said.

"No, he wouldn't ... would he?" Images of Swain's mother laying ill at their house flitted through Fiona's mind. Swain obviously cared deeply about his mom. Would he double-cross them when his mother was in their care?

"I have no idea." Morgan stepped further inside. "This whole case is getting weird."

Fiona and her sisters followed Morgan into the damp interior. Fiona's eyes were pretty well adjusted now and she could see copper plaques on the walls, their faces tinged with green from age.

The smell of damp earth and decaying leaves tickled her nostrils. She stifled a sneeze.

"What now?" Celeste whispered.

"I guess we'll start over there." Morgan pointed to an opening on the north end and they shuffled their way toward it.

Creak!

Fiona whirled around, her heart thudding against her ribcage. The door swung inward behind them, partially blocking the light. When it swung out again, a dark figure blocked the entry.

"Looking for this?" The figure stepped out of the shadow and Fiona could see he was holding the malachite pestle. Her eyes went from the pestle to his face. Her breath caught in her throat. In the doorway stood one of her least favorite people—Sheriff Overton.

***

Sheriff Overton?" Morgan's voice rose in disbelief. "What are you doing here?"

"I'm here for the relic." Overton stepped closer, hitching up his pants over his generous stomach with his free hand, a toothpick dangling out of the right side of his mouth.

"What makes you think we have it?" Morgan asked, and Fiona breathed a sigh of relief that they'd given the mortar to Gordy to take back to the house.

Overton snorted. Do you girls think I'm stupid? I know what you've been up to. I've been checking up on you."

"What makes you think we'd just give it to you?" Jolene asked.

"First of all, it's no good without this." A spark of light from the open doorway glinted off the pestle and threw a shard of green light across the room as Overton dangled it in the air. "And second of all, I have something you want to trade for it." He jerked his head toward the corner.

Something stumbled forward out of the darkness as if it was pushed. Fiona's heart clenched when she saw it was Swain, tied up with rope.

"I'll trade you Mr. Swain, here, for the mortar," Overton said.

"What?" No way. We're not giving up the mortar for him. We don't even know him that well." Jolene's eyes slid over to Swain, who looked cool as a cucumber even though he was tied up like a sack of potatoes. Fiona's eyes locked on his and she noticed his widen, then he dipped his head and extended his hip slightly.

Was he trying to tell her something?

"There's only one mortar and one pestle. We can't *both* have them, so why not just give the mortar to me?" Overton switched the toothpick from the right side of his mouth to the left. "I'll keep it out of Bly's hands *and* hand over Swain in exchange—*after* you get the mortar for me. But I'd decide quickly, or it could get ugly."

Fiona glanced at her sisters. Sure, Overton would keep the relic away from Bly, but his plan for it might be just as objectionable. But they had to get Swain out of his clutches somehow.

Overton shifted his weight impatiently. "You have one minute before I unleash my secret weapon."

Morgan's brows shot up. "Secret weapon?"

A wind gusted from the back of the mausoleum, kicking up a patch of dried leaves that chased each other around in a circle. The wind got stronger and then someone stepped out from behind Swain.

"Wendy!" Morgan gasped.

Wendy smiled, her hair flying out as if caught in the wind. The obsidian pendant dangling from her neck twisted and swirled against her chest.

"You were working with Overton this whole time?" Jolene asked.

Wendy nodded.

"You're not Finch's health aide?" Celeste asked.

"No." Wendy laughed. "You actually fell for that?"

"But why?" Morgan looked from Overton to Wendy and back again.

"I planted her there to keep track of what you girls were up to," Overton said. "At first, it was because we wanted to ask Finch questions, but when we saw that you girls kept coming to see him, we figured you must think he had important information, so we stuck around to find out what it was *you* were asking."

"So, you were the one who stole the pestle from the police evidence," Jolene said.

"Yep. It's pretty easy to appropriate evidence for your own private collection when you are the sheriff." Overton looked at the pestle. "I've had this darn thing for years now, just waiting on the mortar."

"Why wait until now?" Celeste asked. Fiona noticed her sister was inching her way over toward Swain one tiny half-step at a time when Overton's attention was on someone else.

Overton's face flushed. "I didn't know it was in town until recently."

"Where did you think it was?" Jolene had moved an inch toward Swain, too.

"I thought someone had taken it way back when the fire happened. It was assumed that's why the pharmacy was burned in the first place. I thought it was just dumb luck that they didn't get the pestle."

"You never noticed the mortar in the rubble from the pharmacy?" Morgan looked at Overton incredulously. "I thought the police went through it thoroughly."

Overton made a disgusted face. "No. Apparently my deputies weren't very swift back then. Last week, I heard it was in town but didn't know where. The last place I thought it would be was in the rubble from the fire. My boys were supposed to have gone over that with a fine-tooth comb. But once I heard you girls were looking for it, I figured you'd lead the way."

"So you followed us," Fiona said.

"Yep. And I had Wendy here keep you girls in line."

Morgan's brow creased. "Keep us in line? What do you mean? And why did you say she is your secret weapon?"

Wendy laughed and puffed out her cheeks.

A sharp wind ruffled Fiona's hair. It picked up quickly, almost knocking her off balance. Her hair whipped around her face, the ends stinging her cheeks. She grabbed onto the wall and leaned into the wind to steady herself.

"What the heck?" Fiona yelled, but the wind whipped her words away and all she could hear was a roar in her ears and the pounding of her own heart.

The wind stopped abruptly and Fiona stumbled, before correcting herself.

"See?" Overton said smugly. "My friend Wendy here has a way with wind and I amped up her powers with that locket you girls were so nice to give me the last time we crossed paths."

Wendy held up the obsidian amulet. "And thanks to you girls, I have my gifts with the wind to strike out at whoever I want to stop and this amulet to defend me against others' energy."

Fiona almost laughed. Even though Overton had used the meteorite locket to amplify Wendy's powers, the obsidian stones could not be boosted the same way. Wendy might try to use the amulet against them, but she wouldn't get the result she expected.

Morgan turned to Wendy. "So, it was *you* in the graveyard?"

Wendy nodded, inspecting her fingernails nonchalantly.

"But why? Why destroy the gravestone? And why knock Jolene out with the tree limb?"

"I had her destroy the stone to stop you girls from figuring out the last line and beating us to the mortar. I appreciate you girls leading us to it, but we couldn't have you figuring out the last line before we did." Overton frowned. "We couldn't decipher it, though." His face turned happy again.

"Knocking Jolene out was just an unexpected benefit."

Jolene scowled at Overton, her hands fisted on her hips. "I don't get it. If you already knew the clue, why go back to see Finch. Why didn't you just go get the mortar?"

Overton's face darkened. "We knew the epitaph was the clue and we knew the last line, but we misinterpreted it."

"We needed Finch to tell us what that darn line meant," Wendy added.

"And did he?" Fiona asked. She noticed Jolene, Morgan and Celeste seemed to be slowly positioning themselves. The subtle looks they were giving each other told her they were probably trying to send out signals to one another regarding a plan of attack. The sisters weren't telepathic, but they'd been together long enough that they could communicate pretty well with glances and gestures.

Fiona's heart twisted. She felt left out, but since she had no defensive skills, she couldn't really blame them. She was useless. Instinctively, her hand slipped into her pocket and tightened around the stones.

"He didn't," Wendy said. "I tried to coax it out of him medicinally."

"Medicinally?" Morgan looked at her sharply. "You mean that pill you gave him was some kind of truth pill or something?"

Wendy shrugged. "Or something."

"Wait a minute." Celeste narrowed her eyes. "You didn't..."

"Kill him? No. Mr. Finch left us of his own accord." Wendy's eyes darkened. "Unfortunately, that was before he could tell us what we wanted to know. That's why I had to lead you girls here."

"So, this whole time, you've been following our lead," Jolene said. "Letting us do the work and then acting on the clues we found?"

"Yes." Overton puffed up proudly. "Clever, wouldn't you say?"

"So, it was *you* who broke into the museum, then?" Morgan glanced at Swain and Fiona followed her glance. Swain seemed awfully fidgety. Fiona realized that Morgan was keeping Overton talking on purpose to buy them time.

Overton's brows mashed together. "Broke into the museum?"

"Yes. To steal the items from the Finch display. You thought the mortar would be there," Celeste said.

Overton shook his head. "No, that wasn't me. I'd already checked that out when I was sheriff in town, so I knew the mortar wasn't in there."

"If it wasn't you ... then who was it?" Celeste asked.

Bang!

The door flew open. Two large bodies appeared, blocking almost all the light. They stepped slowly aside, revealing a much smaller body which made its way into the mausoleum unhurriedly.

At first, the person was just a dark shadow, but as he moved inside, the light from the door caught the side of his face and Fiona's heart froze as she recognized who it was.

Dr. Mortimer Bly.

"Well, I guess that answers the question," Jolene mumbled.

Not long ago, Dr. Bly had tried to kill her mother and Jolene by draining their energy. Fiona and her sisters, along with Luke, Cal and Jake, had undertaken a mission to rescue the captive Jolene and Johanna and bring them back home. It was no easy task—Bly was powerful and influential with an army of paranormals. The girls had put up quite a fight with their paranormal powers and Fiona felt a momentary triumph to see that Bly still wore an eye patch—the eye had been damaged by their aunt during their earlier run-in. Fiona was glad it had lasting effects. Then again, maybe that wasn't such a good thing because he looked like he was still really pissed at them. And she was sure he was the type to hold a grudge.

Her gaze shifted from Bly to Overton. Ironically, Overton had helped them escape from Bly's headquarters on Fury Rock. Not because of any love for the Blackmoores, though. He did it for his own selfish purposes. Bly was probably pretty mad at him, too.

"Well, well, well. It's great that you're all here." Dr. Bly looked around the room with a satisfied smirk on his face, his glance lingering on Jolene. "It will make it easier to dispose of the bodies after I get what I want."

Chapter Twenty-Four

"And to answer your question ... yes, it was my guys that broke into the museum," Bly continued, indicating the two behemoths on either side of him which Fiona now recognized as two of the bearded guys they'd fought with outside the museum. She didn't dare ask where the third bearded paranormal was. "But the items were worthless! We did, however, find a clue to the cornerstone from one of the items. Too bad when we got there you girls had already been into it ... and ... well ... we all know what happened after that."

The man to the left of Bly—the red-bearded man who Jolene had shot the black goo at—rubbed his scarred face. Bly gave him a quick glance. "I know Raoul here won't forget. And I also know you girls won't be so lucky this time!"

Raoul glared at Jolene and Fiona saw her little sister flex her fingers. Would Jolene's energy gifts work? If not, what chance did they have?

Bly turned his attention to Overton. "And *you*! I should have dealt with you long ago."

"I'm surprised you're still around. I heard the girls here did a number on your headquarters and your little army of paranormals," Overton taunted Bly.

A sour look crossed Bly's face. He glared at Fiona and her sisters. "There was *some* damage. My forces were a bit reduced, but, as you can see, I still have much of my army."

Bly snapped his fingers and two more large figures appeared in the doorway behind him. Fiona's heart swooped. She had been thinking they might be able to beat out the two beards, but with *four* paranormals on Bly's side, the odds were not in the girls' favor.

Bly continued. "And I will rebuild. Especially once I have the relic." He touched the patch on his eye. "In fact, I could use it to heal myself. If you hand over the mortar and pestle now, I might spare some of you."

Bly looked at Overton.

Overton looked at Morgan.

Morgan looked at Jolene.

Jolene looked at Swain.

Fiona's hand tightened around the rocks in her pocket. Her nerves tingled.

"We don't have the mortar here," Morgan said.

"Really? But you *have* it and you can get it, right? I'll just hold one of you hostage to assure it gets to me." Bly turned to Overton. "You, on the other hand—I see you have the pestle. Hand it over now and I'll make your death less painful."

Overton glanced at Wendy. "I don't think so, Bly. I'm done taking orders from you ... Wendy—get them!"

Wendy stepped toward the first two beards, who looked momentarily confused. She pursed her lips and a breeze brushed Fiona's cheek.

The beards looked at each other, then at Bly, then at the two paranormals behind them. The five of them started laughing. "What's that about? You gonna kill us with a breeze?"

Wendy's face grew as dark as storm clouds and she flung her hands out at the laughing paranormals. A roar of wind knocked them backwards, but they regained their footing quickly.

Red-beard fought the wind, advancing slowly on Wendy while large-beard turned his attention toward the Blackmoores, who were busy trying to remain standing and not succumb to the gale-force winds mounting inside the mausoleum. He steadied himself against the concrete wall and pulled something out of his pocket. Fiona recognized it as a small energy laser and her heart clenched when he aimed it directly at Jolene.

Morgan was watching him, too, and jumped in front of Jolene. Her jet-black hair whipped around them like a shroud as she held her amulet out to absorb the energy stream.

Jolene thrust her fingers out. Fiona held her breath. A small bead of yellow energy appeared at the tip of Jolene's index finger. The bead was whipped away harmlessly by the wind. Fiona's stomach sank. Jolene wouldn't be able to help them get out of this.

The wind started to die down. Fiona jerked her head in Wendy's direction and saw red-beard pointing a geode at Wendy. It was zapping her energy. Wendy clutched the obsidian amulet in front of her protectively to ward off the effects of the geode, but Fiona knew it wouldn't work. Fiona would have been happy about this if it wasn't for the other two paranormals—she could see now they didn't have beards—who were advancing on her sisters with some sort of gun held out.

In the corner, Overton's eyes widened as he saw Wendy slumping. "Use the amulet!" he shouted to her, even though she was clearly already using it. Realization dawned on Overton's face and he glared at Fiona. "You gave her a dud!"

She didn't have time to answer him. One of the paranormals aimed his laser at her and fired. She had barely enough time to duck and push her amulet out to ward off the light blue energy stream.

"My pocket!" Swain yelled across the room and Fiona saw Celeste was already running for him. She reached into his pocket and pulled out

232

the mica refractor, just as a stream of purple energy shot toward her from the gun the second non-beard held. She jerked the refractor up into its path. The purple energy hit the mica, then reversed its destination, searing the non-beard in the chest.

"Argh!" He clutched his chest. The laser clattered to the floor as the non-beard's body slumped into a heap.

"Grab the end of the rope," Swain yelled at Celeste, indicating the end of rope sticking out by his hands. She grabbed it and Swain shimmied his body, then the rope unraveled and fell to the ground. Fiona realized he'd been quietly working on getting out of the ropes the whole time.

Fiona looked back toward Overton in time to see him backing slowly into one of the niches. *Did he have an escape route?* She didn't have much time to think about it before the mausoleum burst into a chaotic frenzy of activity.

Red-beard lunged toward Swain with his geode, but Celeste caught him in the elbow with a round-house kick, causing him to drop the geode which rolled along the floor toward the back of the room.

"Get it!" Bly yelled and red-beard dove toward it while still holding his injured elbow. Morgan stuck her foot out, catching him at the ankles. The forward momentum sent him headfirst into the concrete wall and he slumped dazed in the corner.

"Over here!" Morgan called to Fiona, indicating for her to move toward the door where Jolene was warding off a stream of energy from the other non-beard with her amulet. In the back, Celeste kicked out at large-beard before he could aim his geode at Morgan, and Fiona noticed Swain making a beeline for Overton's corner.

Fiona made her way over to Morgan's side, watching Bly out of the corner of her eye. She noticed he wasn't doing much besides barking out orders and a realization hit her. Bly didn't have any paranormal powers of his own.

Somehow during the fight, they'd gone clockwise in a circle. Now, Fiona and her sisters were standing with their backs to the door and Bly and his minions were near the back wall. Wendy was still slumped in the corner. Overton was nowhere to be seen. Fiona was not surprised—it was just like him to sneak off.

Bly's men were starting to recover. The non-beards aimed their lasers at the sisters and Fiona noticed the amulets absorption powers were waning. The stones could only absorb so much energy before they needed to be drained and they were reaching their limit.

Swain had appeared at her side and was using the refractor, but the surface area of the refractor was small and could only be used to defend against one threat ... soon there would be four threats and the power of their amulets would be depleted.

Red-beard had recovered. He picked up the geode and the four paranormals advanced on the sisters. Fiona felt a jolt of panic. They were losing the fight!

"Get the brunette!" Bly directed his minions toward Jolene. Large-beard lunged for Jolene, grabbing her arm roughly and pulling her toward him. Celeste tried to pull her back, but at that moment, her amulet failed and she was hit with a burst of white energy. She went down with a high-pitched shriek that ripped out Fiona's heart.

Panic raced through Fiona's veins. She didn't see any way to beat Bly. Then, a golden light up near the ceiling caught her eye. She looked up, her eyes widening in disbelief. It was impossible ... but there it was—a dragonfly, its iridescent, golden-yellow wings winking in the light as it flew around in a lazy circle.

A dragonfly in November?

And then she realized her hand that held the rocks was burning. She felt a powerful energy moving up her arm and, in that second, she *believed*.

"Get back!" Fiona yelled to her sisters, indicating they should retreat toward the door.

They look at her in confusion as she pulled her hand out of her pocket and raised it in the air.

She sucked in a deep breath. Time stopped. As she raised her arm, she flung the rocks toward Bly's minions and lunged for Jolene's free arm engaging in a tug of war with large-beard as the fiery, red rocks flew out into the room.

One of the larger rocks hit large-beard in between the eyes with a sizzle. Fiona's nose wrinkled at the smell of burning flesh. Large-beard loosened his grip on Jolene and Fiona pulled her away.

The rocks pummeled Bly and his minions, hitting their chests, their arms, their legs and then bouncing off and ricocheting around the mausoleum, only to hit them again. Each rock inflicted a searing burn and elicited shouts of pain from its victim.

They dropped their weapons and the geode so they could use their hands to ward off the bouncing, rebounding, sizzling-hot rocks.

"Let's go!" Morgan flung the door open and they spilled out. Swain, who was last, slammed the door shut behind them.

"Lock it!" Morgan indicated the rusty lock that hung from the ancient hasp on the door.

Fiona could hear the rocks ricocheting off the walls and screams from inside. "But they'll be trapped in there."

Morgan shot her an incredulous look. "Who cares? They tried to kill us."

Swain pushed the lock shut. "They won't be trapped. There's a secret exit. That's where Overton disappeared to."

"We better hurry before they figure it out!" Morgan put her arm around Celeste, who was still reeling from her injury, and they ran for the car.

"The Kia is gone!" Jolene said as they piled into the TrailBlazer.

"Overton must have taken it." Morgan's voice was laced with disappointment. "Which means he got away with the pestle."

"Shoot!" Jolene looked at Morgan. "So this was all for nothing?"

"No, it wasn't," Swain said from the backseat. He pulled something out of his inner vest pocket. Fiona's heart swelled when she saw the green glow … it was the pestle!

"But how did you get it?" Morgan asked.

"While you were all fighting, I had a little altercation with Overton and happened to lift it out of his pocket. I'm not sure he even knows I have it and I think he's going to be right mad when he figures out I pick-pocketed it from him," Swain said slyly.

"Pick-pocketed?" Jolene asked.

"You might not realize it, but you have to master a lot of diverse skills to be an archaeologist

—getting out of ropes and pick-pocketing are just a few," Swain said. "Now, let's get going and put this relic to good use."

Epitaph

Jolene stacked the last of Johanna's fine china into the cabinet. After helping with the cleanup, everyone else had gone off visiting or retired to their rooms. Jolene had volunteered to put away their good dishes, glasses and sliverware, which were all now sitting in the china cabinet waiting for the next holiday. Would they be back in time for Christmas? Jolene hoped so—surely they'd be able to complete their mission before then.

Worry gnawed at her stomach. She wasn't sure what to expect on this new mission. She didn't know anything about the area but the prospect of giant, hungry bugs did not appeal to her. That was the least of her worries, though. If Dorian knew about this relic, that meant that others might, too ... others that wanted the relic for themselves.

She flexed her fingers, straining for that powerful tingle she felt when she was in command of her gifts. Her heart sank—she barely felt anything. Would she be able to help her sisters fight off any paranormal bad guys they encountered in their search for this new relic?

If she didn't get her powers back soon, it could be deadly for the sisters. But she'd *tried* so hard. She'd even taken Fiona's advice about *believing* to heart, but that hadn't worked. It was almost as if something was stuck and she couldn't get her energy pattern started, like a car with a drained battery that needed a jump start.

"*Mawww!*"

Belladonna trotted into the room, looked up at Jolene and jerked her head toward the front door seconds before Jolene heard a noise at the door. She walked down the front hall to investigate. Mateo stood at the front door, his black duffel bag packed and ready to go.

"You're leaving?" Jolene wondered why she felt so disappointed.

"Yep, I'm heading out ahead of you." Mateo let the bag slip from his shoulder to the floor. "I'm your recon man. Not that you girls need help, judging by the way you handled Bly. You seem to be doing fine without me."

Jolene frowned, thinking of the times before she'd mastered her gifts that Mateo had mysteriously appeared just when she needed him most. It felt good to have someone watching her back. "I think we can always use an extra hand. We beat Bly in the mausoleum, but it was close."

He laughed. "Don't worry. If I thought you guys needed me, I would have been there. Fiona just had to believe and maybe you do, too."

Jolene signed and shifted on her feet. "Yeah, I tried that ..."

He slipped his thumb under her chin, tilting her head up so she was forced to look into his velvety eyes.

"Don't worry, it will come back." His lips were disturbingly close to hers, causing her heart to thud loudly. "Sometimes it just takes an extra push. A little magic."

Jolene felt a rush of energy as his lips brushed against hers, softly at first, and then his arm snaked around her waist and he pulled her close, his lips becoming more demanding, the fingers of his other hand lacing with hers.

She must have forgotten how to breathe because she felt light-headed, like the room was spinning. Her lips tingled and the tingling didn't stop there, either.

Wait ... tingling?

The tingling got stronger and she recognized it as that feeling of energy she used to get when her gifts were working properly. The energy traveled from her lips, to her chest and then down her arm to her fingertips.

She pulled away from him, disentangled her fingers from his and stared down at them wide-eyed. "Hey, it feels like ..."

Mateo had already hefted the duffel bag onto his shoulder and had the door open. He smiled down at her.

"Yep, I think you guys are going to be okay without me." He winked, then slipped out the door, closing it gently behind him.

Jolene stared at the closed door, then looked down at her hand, feeling the powerful tingling that she'd feared was gone forever. What had just happened?

Had Mateo given her her gift back?

She put her hand out in front of her and concentrated on her fingertips. She felt a powerful, hot energy gathering, and then she thrust her fingers out.

A glowing stream of red energy shot out toward her mother's favorite crystal lamp.

"Shoot!" She tried to pull the energy back, but it was too late.

Crash!

The lamp exploded, sending shards of glass all over the living room.

"Is everything okay down there?" Johanna's concerned voice shouted from the upstairs hallway.

Jolene grimaced. She didn't look forward to explaining this to her mother. But then she looked down at her hand and couldn't help but smile. She had her gifts back and everything else paled in comparison.

"Don't worry, Mom," she yelled back up. "I think everything is going to be just fine."

The End.

***

Want more Blackmoore Sisters adventures? Buy the rest of the books in the series for your Kindle:

Dead Wrong (Book 1)
Dead & Buried (Book 2)
Dead Tide (Book 3)
Buried Secrets (Book 4)
Deadly Intentions (Book 5)

Sign up for my newsletter and find out how to get my latest releases at the lowest discount price:

http://www.leighanndobbs.com/newsletter

If you want to receive a text message on your cell phone when I have a new release, text COZYMYSTERY to 88202 (sorry, this only works for US cell phones!)

Author's Note

I hope you enjoyed reading this book as much as I enjoyed writing it. This is the sixth book in the Blackmoore Sisters mystery series and I have a whole bunch more planned!

The setting for this book series is based on one of my favorite places in the world – Ogunquit, Maine. Of course, I changed some of the geography around to suit my story, and changed the name of the town to Noquitt but the basics are there. Anyone familiar with Ogunquit will recognize some of the landmarks I have in the book.

The house the sisters live in sits at the very end of Perkins Cove and I was always fascinated with it as a kid. Of course, back then it was a mysterious, creepy old house that was privately owned and I was dying to go in there. I'm sure it must have had an attic stuffed full of antiques, just like in the book!

Today, it's been all modernized and updated— I think you can even rent it out for a summer vacation. In the book, the house looks different and it's also set high up on a cliff (you'll see why in a later book) where in real life it's not. I've also made the house much older to suit my story.

Also, if you like this book, you might like my Mystic Notch series which is set in the White

Mountains of New Hampshire and filled with magic and cats. I have an excerpt from the first book "Ghostly Paws" at the end of this book.

This book has been through many edits with several people and even some software programs, but since nothing is infallible (even the software programs) you might catch a spelling error or mistake and, if you do, I sure would appreciate it if you let me know - you can contact me at lee@leighanndobbs.com.

Oh, and I love to connect with my readers so please do visit me on Facebook at http://www.facebook.com/leighanndobbsbooks or at my website http://www.leighanndobbs.com.

Are you signed up to get notifications of my latest releases and special contests? Go to: http://www.leighanndobbs.com/newsletter and enter your email address to signup - I promise never to share it and I only send emails every couple of weeks so I won't fill up your inbox.

If you want to receive a text message on your cell phone when I have a new release, text COZYMYSTERY to 88202 (sorry, this only works for US cell phones!)

About The Author

USA Today best-selling Author, Leighann Dobbs, has had a passion for reading since she was old enough to hold a book, but she didn't put pen to paper until much later in life. After a twenty-year career as a software engineer, with a few side trips into selling antiques and making jewelry, she realized you can't make a living reading books, so she tried her hand at writing them and discovered she had a passion for that, too! She lives in New Hampshire with her husband, Bruce, their trusty Chihuahua mix, Mojo, and beautiful rescue cat, Kitty.

Find out about her latest books and how to get discounts on them by signing up at:

http://www.leighanndobbs.com/newsletter

If you want to receive a text message alert on your cell phone for new releases , text COZYMYSTERY to 88202 (sorry, this only works for US cell phones!)

Connect with Leighann on Facebook
http://facebook.com/leighanndobbsbooks

More Books By Leighann Dobbs:

Mooseamuck Island
Cozy Mystery Series
* * *

A Zen For Murder

Mystic Notch
Cat Cozy Mystery Series
* * *

Ghostly Paws
A Spirited Tail

Blackmoore Sisters
Cozy Mystery Series
* * *

Dead Wrong
Dead & Buried
Dead Tide
Buried Secrets
Deadly Intentions

Lexy Baker
Cozy Mystery Series
* * *

Lexy Baker Cozy Mystery Series Boxed Set Vol 1
(Books 1-4)

Or buy the books separately:

Killer Cupcakes
Dying For Danish
Murder, Money and Marzipan
3 Bodies and a Biscotti

Brownies, Bodies & Bad Guys
Bake, Battle & Roll
Wedded Blintz
Scones, Skulls & Scams
Ice Cream Murder
Mummified Meringues

Kate Diamond
Adventure/Suspense Series
* * *

Hidden Agemda

Dobbs "Fancytales"
Regency Romance Fairytales Series
* * *

Something In Red
Snow White and the Seven Rogues
Dancing On Glass
The Beast of Edenmaine
The Reluctant Princess
Sleeping Heiress

Contemporary
Romance
* * *

Sweet Escapes
Reluctant Romance

Excerpt From Ghostly Paws

In over thirty years as head librarian for the Mystic Notch Library, Lavinia Babbage had never once opened the doors before eight a.m.

I knew this because my bookstore sat across the street and three doors down from the library. Every day, I passed its darkened windows on my way to work. I watched Lavinia turn on the lights and open the doors every single morning at precisely eight a.m. from inside my shop.

Most days I didn't pay much attention to the library, though. It was really the last thing on my mind as I walked past, my mind set on sorting through a large box of books I'd purchased at an estate sale earlier in the week. The edges of my lips curled in a smile as I thought about the gold placard I'd had installed on the oak door of the old bookshop just the day before. *Wilhelmina Chance, Proprietor*. That made things official—the shop was mine and I was back in my hometown, Mystic Notch, to stay.

I hurried down the street, deep in my own thoughts. The early morning mist, which wrapped itself around our sleepy town in the White Mountains of New Hampshire, had caused the pain to flare in my leg, and I forced myself not to limp. I continued along, my head down and engrossed in my thoughts when I nearly tripped over something gray and furry. My cat, Pandora, had stopped short in front of me causing me to do a painful sidestep to avoid squashing her.

"Hey, what the heck?"

Pandora blinked her golden-green eyes at me and jerked her head toward the library ... or at least it seemed like she did. Cats didn't actually jerk their heads toward things, though, did they?

Of course they didn't.

I looked in the direction of the library anyway. That's when I noticed the beam of light spilling onto the granite steps from the half-open library door.

Which was odd, since it was only ten past seven.

My stomach started to feel queasy. Lavinia never opened up this early. Should I venture in to check it out? Maybe Lavinia had come in early to catch up on restocking the bookshelves before the library opened. But she never left the door open like that. She was as strict as a nun about keeping that door closed.

I stood on the sidewalk, staring at the medieval-looking stone library building, my pre-caffeine fog making it difficult for me to decide what to do.

Pandora had no such trouble deciding. She raced up the steps past me. With a flick of her gray tail, she darted toward the massive oak door, shooting a reproachful look at me over her shoulder before disappearing into the building.

I took a deep breath and followed her inside.

"Lavinia? You in here?" My words echoed inside the library as I pushed the heavy oak door open, its hinges groaning eerily. The library was as still as a morgue with only the sound of the grandfather clock marking time in the corner broke the silence.

"Lavinia? You okay?"

No one answered.

I crept past the old oak desk, stacked with books ready to return to the library shelves. The bronze bust of Franklin Pierce, fourteenth president of the United States, glared at me from the end of the hall. I didn't have a good feeling about this.

"Meow." The sound came from the back corner where the stone steps lead to the lower level. Dammit! I'd warned Lavinia about those steps. They were steep and she wasn't that steady on her feet anymore.

I headed toward the back, my heart sinking as I noticed Lavinia's cane lying at the top of the stairs.

"Lavinia?" Rounding the corner, my stomach dropped when I saw a crumpled heap at the bottom of the stairs ... Lavinia.

I raced down the steps two at a time, my heart pounding as I took in the scene. Blood on the steps. Lavinia laying there, blood in her gray hair. She'd fallen and taken it hard on the way down. But she could still be alive.

I bent down beside her, taking her wrist between my fingers and checking for a pulse.

Lavinia's head tilted at a strange angle. Her glassy eyes stared toward the room where she kept new book arrivals before cataloguing them. I dropped her wrist, ending my search for a pulse.

Lavinia Babbage had stamped her last library book.

***

I called my sister Augusta, or Gus as I called her, who also happened to be the sheriff, and sat on the steps to wait. I might have drifted off, still sleepy from the lack of caffeine, because the next thing I heard was Augusta's voice in my ear.

"Willa, are you okay?"

I opened one eye to the welcome sight of the steaming Styrofoam coffee cup that Gus was holding out to me.

"I'm fine," I said, reaching for the cup.

"What happened?" I studied Gus who stood on the steps in front of me. No one would have guessed we were sisters. She was petite, her long, straight blonde hair tied back in a ponytail, which, I assume, she thought made her look more sheriff-like. Even in the un-flattering sheriff's uniform, you could tell she had an almost perfect hourglass figure. I was tall with thick wavy red hair, my figure more rounded—voluptuous, as some described me. The only thing we had in common was our amber colored eyes—same as our mom's.

"I was on my way to open the bookstore when I noticed the lights on in the library." I glanced down the street toward the municipal parking lot.

Now that the spring warm-up was here, I was trying to work in some extra exercise by parking in the lot two blocks away instead of on the street near the bookstore.

"Was that unusual?" Gus asked.

"Yep." I looked over my shoulder at the front door of the library. "It sure was. Lavinia never opens the library before eight. Plus the front door was cracked open, and she never leaves it open."

Gus started up the steps toward the library. "Did you touch anything?"

I stood up, wincing at the pain in my left leg—a reminder of the near fatal accident over a year ago that was one of the catalysts for my move back to Mystic Notch. The accident had left me with a slight limp, a bunch of scars and a few odd side effects I didn't like to dwell on.

"Nope, other than Lavinia. I didn't know if she was alive and needed aid," I said as I followed Gus into the library.

Gus stopped just inside the door and looked around. The coppery smell of blood tinged the air, making me lose interest in my coffee.

"It doesn't seem like anything is out of place ... no sign of struggle," she said.

"Nope, I think she just fell down the stairs." I started toward the back. "You know she was getting on in years and not that steady on her feet."

We turned the corner and my stomach clenched at the sight of Lavinia at the bottom of the steps.

"That's her cane?" Gus pointed to the purple metal cane, which was still lying as I'd found it.

"Yep. Looks like she lost her balance, dropped the cane, and fell."

Gus descended the stairs, her eyes carefully taking in every detail. She knelt beside Lavinia, studying her head. "She's pretty banged up."

"I know. These stairs are hard stone. I guess they can do a number on you." I winced as I looked at the bloody edges of the steps.

"So, you think this was an accident?"

"Sure. I mean, what else could have happened?"

"Yeah, you're probably right. No reason to suspect foul play." Gus stood and looked back up the stairs, down the hall and then back at Lavinia.

Her lips were pressed in a thin line and I wondered what she was thinking. I knew she was a good cop, but the truth was I didn't really know her all that well. Eight years separated us and she was just a teenager when I'd moved down south. Now, twenty-five years later, we were just becoming acquainted as adults.

"Mew." Pandora sat on the empty table in the storage room where Lavinia temporarily stored new books or returns before she catalogued them. I'd forgotten she was here. She wasn't really my cat ... well, not until recently. I'd inherited her along with the bookstore and my grandmother's house. I still wasn't used to being followed around by a feline.

"Isn't that Pandora?" Gus asked. Gus had been close to grandma—closer than I had, and it was somewhat of a mystery that Grandma had left me the shop, her house and the cat. In her will, she'd said she'd wanted me to come back home and have a house and business, which was odd because the timing had been perfect. She'd left a tidy sum of money for Gus, so at least there were no hard feelings.

"Yeah, she rides to work with me."

Gus raised a brow at me, but didn't say anything. Pandora stared at us—her intelligent, greenish-gold eyes contrasting eerily with her sleek gray fur.

"So, if it was unusual for Lavinia to be here at this time of the morning, why do you think she was here and what do you think she was doing?" Gus asked.

"I'm not sure."

Gus reached out to pet Pandora, who still sat on the table staring at us. "Are there any mice in here, Pandora? Maybe Lavinia heard something down here and wanted to investigate."

"Maybe." I looked around the floor for evidence of mice. Lavinia ran a pretty tight ship so I doubted there would be any mice in the library. And, since the room was empty of books, she hadn't come in early to catalogue new arrivals.

Which begged the question ... why *was* Lavinia in the library this early in the first place?

10785971R00142

Printed in Great Britain
by Amazon.co.uk, Ltd.,
Marston Gate.